Clang

THE RILEY BROTHERS BOOK 2

E. DAVIES

Publisher's Note: This is a work of fiction. Names, characters, places, and incidents are a product of the author's imagination. Locales and public names are sometimes used for atmospheric purposes. Any resemblance to actual people, living or dead, or to businesses, companies, events, institutions, or locales is completely coincidental.

Clang / E. Davies. – 2nd ed.
ISBN: 978-1-912245-01-7

CHAPTER
One

JACKSON

The best sound in the world was a sizzle. To Jackson Riley, it meant hot metal gripped in his tongs and plunged into a barrel of water.

Jackson smiled. He lifted the rod and flipped his hand over. As he dipped the other end into the barrel, the last few inches of metal cooled. This was the last railing of the night; it was getting late. He worked from his suburban backyard workshop, which was covered in ordinances. He'd modified his anvil to deaden the sound, but his workday had to be over at 9 p.m..

Now, he had to decide what to do for supper.

He clamped one end, then twisted the railing around and hammered the other end. The twisted rods bent out and he shaped them with ease. The metal was quite cool by the time he finished flattening the smooth, flowing stems. He dunked the metal again and set it down to finish tomorrow.

Now that he lived next to his two brothers and worked in his backyard, there were certain perks. For one, he didn't have to run back and forth to his workshop to get measurements for the custom work he was doing for his brothers.

Right now, he was working on custom wrought iron railings for his little brother, Cameron. Cam's house had a vaulted ceiling over the living room, and the old railing overlooking it was... ugly. Jackson was creating new railings with his signature twisting, flowing, graceful patterns.

After raking the coals out and sprinkling water on them, Jackson pulled up a chair at the workshop bench. He had to wait for them to finish cooling. His own projects were still in the sketching stages, and he worked on them whenever he had a few minutes, such as now.

He liked the idea of swirls and metal beads molded into the balusters. He'd done a few custom railings for home builders, a few months ago, with an onion effect; he'd liked that, too. He was trying to combine them into something that was not too showy yet highlighted his skills. The sketchbook was full of ideas, none of which had quite worked perfectly.

"Ah, fuck it," he finally muttered and flipped the book shut. He waved a hand over the coals, then raked them again to make sure there were no remaining sparks.

Jackson walked through the grass to the back door of his house. The lights were off at Cam's, so he was probably at Noah's place. Thomas's bedroom light was on but the main floor was off. *Reading in bed again, I bet. Nerd.* He smiled to himself.

Once Jackson was inside, he fumbled with the light switch to illuminate the kitchen.

Burgers? No, he'd done those on the barbecue with his brothers for supper yesterday. Rice and chicken breast? Too much effort.

Jackson pulled open the fridge to look over his options. He had leftover pasta salad and chicken wings. That would do. It was too late to cook a full meal.

He dumped everything onto a plate and put it into the microwave, then sank onto the kitchen stool to wait.

Except for the whir of the microwave and the kitchen clock ticking, the house was quiet and dark. He didn't bother to get up and turn on more lights yet. He was heading straight to bed after supper and maybe a TV show.

Jackson's brothers had moved back to town three months ago now. Some things had changed over the summer, but others hadn't. Being around Cameron and Noah made it hard to ignore his bachelor status.

"Bachelor for life," he murmured as the microwave dinged its completion. He grabbed his plate and utensils to sit at the kitchen island. That usually didn't sound so bad, but now and then...

He moved to the living room to switch on the TV.

CHAPTER

Two

CHASE

"OH, MAN," CHASE YAWNED, RAISING THE BACK OF HIS HAND to cover a yawn. He pressed the end of the pen into his lip as he gazed down at his sketchbook, flicking his tongue along the tip. When he closed his lips and sucked, it took him a few moments to clue in to what he was doing.

God, I need to get laid.

It had been days, but he'd been working overtime all week.

He added a few more swirls of ink with his pen before pushing the sketchbook back. That looked like a fine rough draft.

It was a blocky tattoo of deep black swirls and geometric shapes. This customer had first asked for the same old gross "tribal tattoos" as everyone else. Finally, the guy had agreed to consider something in a similar aesthetic.

Chase hoped he could talk him into this design instead. It would look great on his body shape. A lot of guys around here just didn't understand why asking for "a tribal tattoo" was so fucking gross. Chase hated doing tattoos that made him uncomfortable. He couldn't turn the job down easily, though. He needed more in his new portfolio, and he didn't call the shots at this shop. He'd have to have a word with Floyd.

Small-town New Brunswick.

He sighed, fidgeting with the pen a few more times. He tossed it aside on the desk and leaned back to stretch out his back. Chase's gaze wandered around the shop: glass cabinets he'd polished twice today, a bright waiting room, and no sketchy ads. He'd gotten a job at a pretty good place, all things considered.

And there *were* good jobs. This girl had come in looking for some fun flower watercolors. He was looking forward to getting a chance to work on those. That was a lot closer to his preferred style, but he'd do whatever paid the bills until he built up another portfolio.

Fuck, his chest still burned when he thought about his old portfolio. Hours – hundreds of hours – spent building that up.

It was all gone.

He ground his teeth, checked his watch, and went to lock the door of the shop. Microwave mac and cheese was calling to him.

Three

JACKSON

"Yo, little bro'. Ready to go? Get this show on the road?"

Cameron groaned from the landing at the top of his staircase. "Never rap, please."

Jackson just grinned and jerked a thumb over his shoulder. "Don't keep your boyfriend waiting."

"Yeah, hold on a sec."

Jackson leaned on the front door frame of Cam's place. His gaze wandered up to the shoddy wooden railings overlooking the vaulted living room. He was looking forward to ripping out and replacing those. It would make the house feel much more like the Toronto loft aesthetic he knew Cam was going for.

His little brother came thundering down the stairs two at a time and jumped on the landing. He was looking good, in a black collared shirt with a few little flowers printed on it, and dark jeans. Cameron had chosen shiny brown boots that matched his belt.

Cam looked thinner, too. Upon his diagnosis, they'd all

realized how lucky Cam was to make it through his pro-sports career without cardiac arrest. His condition, CPVT, was usually spotted in young teens or kids. The fact that he'd made it until now was nothing short of a miracle.

Needless to say, they'd forbidden him from exercising. Beta-blockers weren't good enough on their own. The family was preparing for surgery soon, while Cam was still in shape and likely to recover fast. Cam was losing muscle, and it was hard not to notice.

Jackson tried to drag his thoughts away from the worries that had haunted him over the summer. "Noah's done a number on your wardrobe," he teased.

"What?"

"Floral print?"

Cameron rolled his eyes. "Apparently they're "in" this summer."

Jackson laughed and stepped back so Cameron could lock up. It was mid-August and still warm, so they didn't need jackets for the quick walk. They were heading to the bar downtown to catch up with friends.

Thomas didn't usually come out with them, but Cameron often did, and so did his friends. Noah's friends joined in now and then. They'd become a loose friendship group of mostly guys who went out for drinks once or twice a week.

Noah, Cam's boyfriend, was good for him, at least. He made sure Cam got out of the house to socialize, and Cam had loosened up about his condition a lot.

"How was work?"

"Oh, god," Cameron complained. "I can't bend over."

Jackson raised his eyebrows, deadpan. "Noah was working with you today?"

"No, I – fuck off," Cam groaned and smacked Jackson's

shoulder. "I was taking honey off the hives. It's fuckin' heavy. You're disgusting."

Jackson just laughed and elbowed Cam in return. They strode down to the sidewalk, and crossed the street. "You're always out at his place these days."

"Yeah. It's getting annoying going back and forth between our places."

Jackson cast a sideways glance at Cam. Was he hinting at Noah moving in...? Maybe to help with his recovery? Jackson didn't even want to think of that yet, though. "When's his lease up?"

"November." Cam shoved his hands in his pockets. "We've been talking about it."

"Nice," Jackson nodded. "The two of you are... well, it's been three months already, huh?"

"Three and a half." Cameron waited at the crosswalk with Jackson, glancing back at him now. "Yeah... it'd be six months when his lease is up. So..."

"Six months isn't too soon. As long as you feel ready."

"I am. I think he is, too."

Jackson smiled and clapped Cameron's arm as they crossed the street to the bar. "Good for you, man."

"So--"

No way. Jackson went on as if he hadn't heard Cameron beginning to form the dreaded question in response. "Kevin's coming tonight, huh? Ryan said he'd be here too."

Cameron paused, then went on. He opened the door for Jackson and glanced inside. "Looks like Kevin's already here."

Kevin, the captain of Noah's casual hockey club was always up for a drink. He was a house painter and university student heading into his last year of school.

"Hey, man." Ryan came up behind them, clapping both of

them on the back. He worked as a carpentry apprentice. "I've got this round. Just Kevin here?"

"Oh, don't mind, it's only me," Kevin laughed.

"I didn't mean that," Ryan snorted. "The usual?"

"Yeah, thanks."

"I'll help," Jackson offered, walking up to the bar to help carry back beer bottles, plus a Coke for Cam. "Noah's supposed to be here any time now, too. I haven't heard from anyone else yet, but we'll just see who shows up."

"Fair enough. How was your week?"

"Ohhh, so many pieces. I got an order of three hundred rails."

Ryan shrugged. "Whatever pays, eh? Who's it from?"

Jackson took a couple open beer bottles when they were handed over. "Derek – the guy who's in charge of the new subdivision from Frontier Homes."

"Oh, yeah, I know him. He seems all right." Ryan handed over cash with a nod of thanks to the bartender and grabbed the other three.

As Jackson caught up on his week, his gaze wandered back to Cameron. "He told you the news yet?"

"No? I don't think so," Ryan answered. "What is it?"

"I'll tell you at the table."

They slid in moments later, just as Noah came in. He always swished his way around, a bit like Thomas. His mannerisms made Jackson smile fondly.

A quick glance at his brother showed him looking just as enchanted as ever. Cameron's eyes lit up as he stood up to greet his boyfriend with a kiss and pull a chair out for him. Noah wore a vest and collared shirt and tie – he'd been curating some art show or another, then.

"Hi, guys," Noah greeted. He took his beer with a smile and sipped it. He managed not to wince. "Thanks."

Jackson chuckled. Noah didn't really drink beer, but around the guys he made an exception for bonding purposes. "Thank Ryan."

"Nah," Ryan waved it off. "So Cam has news?"

Cameron sank back into his chair, his expression tighter as he grabbed his bottle of Coke. Since going on beta-blockers, he was banned from drinking. "I got the letter with my surgery date."

"Oh, shit," Kevin exclaimed. He didn't know the full extent of Cameron's undiagnosed heart condition. That May, he'd come home from Toronto just as he'd been on the verge of being drafted. When he'd bowed out of the hockey club Kevin captained, Cam had dropped hints. Everyone knew he was waiting on surgery.

Noah smiled, glancing back at Cameron. "He's been waiting for months now. The specialist okayed him. It's been hell with all the specialists deciding what exactly he needs done and where..."

"I bet," Ryan frowned. "Good job, man. When is it?"

"December."

Noah added, "I still can't believe they won't get him in sooner..." For once, he looked pissed, his dark brows drawing together protectively.

"I was lucky even to get all those specialist appointments over the summer," Cameron reminded Noah. He rubbed his boyfriend's arm. "I got ahead of a lot of people." He glanced at the others. "It's an obscure procedure, they told me. Takes a real pro to do it, and there's only a couple in the country."

Noah loosened his tie, the fight going out of him. "Right."

"How long does recovery take?" Ryan asked.

"Hard to say," Cameron answered, his jaw tight. "The first couple months are riskiest. I can't exercise hard. Even afterward... that depends."

"Damn," Kevin shook his head. "And I was just getting used to telling people we got a pro on our team." That broke the mood a little and everyone chuckled. "Glad you're getting treatment finally, though, man. My partner took *months* to get specialist referrals..."

As the others lapsed into conversation about the health-care system, Jackson's mind wandered again. He kept glancing at Cameron and Noah. They'd scooted their chairs closer together so their arms touched. Noah reached out to play with Cameron's hair now and then or adjust his collar.

Jackson's heart squeezed with yearning. Maybe he should get dating... but every gay guy he knew here just wasn't a fit. But there could be some who just didn't hang out with his crowd of beer-loving, hockey-playing guys.

Online dating could be an option.

Hell with it, maybe he'd meet someone new and... get some stress out. Best-case scenario, he could get a date or two. Hanging out with friends was fine, but he had to avoid becoming a romantic hermit.

"What am I doing?" Jackson groaned as he leaned back in his computer chair. His small office was covered in paperwork for his business, but he kept one desk clear for his computer.

He was going to have to bring his laptop to the couch and brainstorm.

Once he settled on the couch in the living room, Jackson opened his profile again and stared at it.

What defined him? What would men find appealing, aside from the blacksmith thing? That *did* get him a lot of attention, and he wasn't ashamed to admit it was kind of nice. But what would be interesting about the rest of him?

He bit his lip. *Perpetual bachelor blacksmith who puts his family first? Not a great line.*

Jackson wrote something to that effect: he was looking for fun dates and maybe settling down with the right guy. He wrote that he put family and his partner first, but that his blacksmithing work was also important to him.

It seemed so bare compared to the profiles he'd glanced over already. Everyone interesting had stuff to say about their job or their hobbies. The guys with bare profiles didn't catch his eye, and he knew they'd look at his bare profile the same way.

He couldn't ask his brothers. That would be way too weird. Someone who knew him loosely but without much of a personal connection...

Chase?

Jackson tried to ignore the flip-flop in his stomach. Chase was a relatively new and gorgeous friend, but he'd never shown a hint of interest in Jackson.

They went out for coffee every few weeks to hang out and bitch about their respective arts jobs that weren't counted as artistic by enough people. Chase was a tattoo artist, and he did damn good work... but most people just didn't understand what went into it. And Chase was gay, so he knew what men were looking for.

He pulled out his phone to send Chase a text.

Hey :) Wanna meet up for coffee soon? I need your opinions on dating.

Moments later, he had his answer.

Someone WANTS my opinions? OMG. ;) Tomorrow at 4?

Jackson grinned.

Works great. See you then.

They might only be casual friends, but it would be nice to get out of the workshop a little early. Jackson shut the laptop without a second thought and turned his attention to the TV.

Four

CHASE

OH, BOY, WAS CHASE READY TO COMPLAIN ABOUT ALL THE asshole guys in town. If Jackson had dating questions, he had more than enough answers.

Jackson was buff and gorgeous, but he always acted restrained around Chase. He was one of the few guys around here who'd never hit on him. Well, he'd flirted a little when they'd met at an art show that spring, but since then... nothing. It was kind of a nice change, if disconcerting.

They vented together about being on the fringe of the arts scene and gay scene and shared stories of their work. Each of them was interested in the other. Blacksmithing and tattooing were totally different but both pretty unique arts professions.

If only Jackson wanted more than casual friendship with him.

He'd expected to bitch about flaky guys, but Jackson caught him off-guard. "Wait... What? You want to *start* online dating?"

Jackson nodded, cradling his white coffee mug by his

chest. He wore his uniform: a dark gray t-shirt that hugged his pecs and stretched around his biceps. Fucking hell, he looked hot. Chase had done a good job pretending not to stare, or so he hoped. "I haven't really done it. I tried a few years ago but all I got were hookups."

Chase smirked. "Such innocence. So why do you need my help?"

Jackson snorted in laughter. "I need help figuring out what to say so I get a boyfriend, not horny guys."

"That's a tall order. I look like the love guru?"

"Nothing says he can't be a tattooed weirdo."

"Hey," Chase grinned. He sipped his coffee and winked. "I'm only freaky in bed. I'm quite normal the rest of the time. I can twist into all kinds of shapes, if it helps--"

"Yeah, yeah," Jackson waved him off with another laugh. "*Anyway*, what do I say?"

"Just be honest, man. You seem pretty down-to-earth. I mean, your brothers know you better... Why not ask them?"

Jackson winced and glanced down into his mug. "Um... embarrassed, I guess."

It was almost hilarious to see a big guy who could lift Chase off his feet one-handed looking so bashful. It was kind of adorable in a heartthrob way, too. Chase took pity on him and grinned instead of laughing. "Why? Everyone dates online now."

"Well, Cameron met Noah in person... Thomas doesn't really date, but... I don't know. It seems sketchy. I haven't even dated in ages."

"Why now? Seeing Cam and Noah around?"

Jackson shook his head. "I don't know. I'm just lonely."

That made Chase pause, the smile fading from his face at the raw admission. They weren't exactly best buddies, so he hadn't heard Jackson talk that way. *He must need my help bad.*

"I get it," Chase assured him after a few moments. "Me, too. I've only got a few friends in the area, even having lived here for months now. One of them's the guy who owns the tattoo shop... The others are pretty much his friends."

Jackson looked sympathetic. "Yeah. I'm lucky I've got buddies around here. Just none of them I want to... you know, romance," he laughed.

Chase chuckled. "All right. You got a computer with you?" He didn't see a jacket or bag.

"Nah, only at home. D'you wanna come back with me?"

"Sure," Chase agreed. For once, the implications weren't sexual. "I'll help you write your profile and woo all the knights in shining armor... armor that needs hammering. Heh..."

Jackson kicked him and laughed. "Shut up."

As they finished their coffee, Chase's mind wandered. *How can a guy with a big family in the city, all those friends, and everyone he knows through work be lonely?*

Maybe he was just trying to take pity on Chase by offering him a hand of friendship. Hell, that was fine by Chase. He got to spend more time around the hunk, even if it was setting him up with someone who wasn't, well... *him!*

"I think that should get some interesting messages. Fill those blanks in."

Chase stretched his fingers and pushed the laptop back to Jackson. He watched him read his profile. It wasn't much –

just a few sentences in each profile box – but it would get him started.

He'd already had to ask Jackson some questions, and the answers were interesting. Of the six most important things to him, Jackson's list was predictable. He'd said family, going out with friends, his blacksmithing work, and great home-cooked food. He'd thought for a moment before adding sunrises. Chase had pressed him for a sixth item and Jackson's thoughtful answer was, "A relationship when the time is right."

That answer was still bouncing around Chase's mind. When the time is right? That didn't sound at all desperate – it sounded like he was happy to wait for years longer, if he had to. Not like Chase.

Jackson skimmed the profile. "This... this sounds decent. Wow." He pointed at the screen. "Want to meet up for 'blank'?"

"I'm assuming you're not gonna put 'casual sex' in there," Chase grinned. "Coffee or a beer or whatever."

"A beer sounds weird. Alcohol on a first date. How about coffee?" Jackson typed that in. He mumbled under his breath as he filled in the other blanks. Chase left it to him to think of a hobby he wanted to share, his greatest secret, and what he was looking for in a man.

He looked cute from this angle. Jackson hunched over the coffee table with his broad shoulders stooped enough to lean down and see the screen. His shirt rose up his back, sliding up enough to leave an inch or two of bare, tattoo-free skin.

Chase clamped down on his moment of arousal.

"Thanks," Jackson concluded as he straightened up.

"Hey, it was only a few sentences here and there." Chase pulled his gaze off Jackson's body and back to his face to make eye contact. *Stop ogling him, Jesus. You'll make things weird.*

"You wanna have supper with me and my brothers?"

Chase didn't have anywhere else to be, and he was running low on freezer meals. "Sure. Thanks. When?"

"Anytime I head outside and turn on the barbecue," Jackson laughed. "They'll smell it."

Chase laughed, too. That sounded nice. "Barbecue? Burgers?"

"Yeah, burgers and steak and veggies. We've come up with a bunch of new recipes. Corn, salad, pizza, pineapple, asparagus, donuts..."

"Salad?" Chase laughed. "Pineapple? Donuts? I mean, corn and asparagus are kinda normal..."

Jackson winked. "Just for that, we're having salad to start and pineapple for dessert. C'mon." Jackson walked to his kitchen, and Chase found himself naturally following.

There was something about him that was just magnetic.

Jackson lit the barbecue first. They chatted more as they cut lettuce heads and defrosted burgers. Chase shucked the corn, his chest aching at the memories of shucking corn for family dinners.

By the time the ingredients were ready, there was a knock on the back door and it slid open.

"Oh, hey," Cameron greeted, raising a hand in greeting to Chase. "What's up?"

Chase had only met him twice. First had been at the same art show where he and Jackson had met. Jackson had sculpted this gorgeous metal statue based on Cameron. It still stood in the arena lobby. Then, Cameron bought Chase's art piece for his living room. It was a collection of miniature paintings done on a series of hockey pucks stuck together with needles. Chase was glad someone had loved it enough to buy it.

"Not much. How're the paintings looking?"

"C'mon over later and I'll show you," Cameron invited. "Noah found the perfect spot for it in the living room. I really like it, man, no bullshit. He makes good stuff." He reached out to shake hands again in greeting as he moved past Chase to his brother.

"He does," Jackson agreed.

Chase grinned. It was nice to hear from someone who appreciated the work he'd put into it. Usually, his art was done with needles and ended up on people's bodies.

"Thomas just got home. He'll be out in a few," Cam told them.

Jackson nodded. "Great. Carry this shit out for me, huh?" He handed Cam a plastic bin filled with barbecue tools.

"Sure, get me to do the heavy lifting," Cameron groaned. He pretended to struggle to haul the box outside.

Chase laughed. Cameron wasn't as muscled as Jackson, but he was pretty built himself. He looked a bit thinner than when they'd last met, though, and he was a little more on-edge.

"Can you take the corn out?"

"Yep." Chase carried the bucket of corn cobs outside to the table next to the barbecue where Cam was setting up the tools. "How's work going?" he asked Cameron. He remembered Jackson mentioning he was a beekeeper, but he didn't know anything else.

"Oh, busy this time of year," Cameron admitted. "My boss gave me the day off to see the doctor."

Ahh, there is something up with him. Aw. "Yeah? Must be good to have a break."

Cameron nodded. "I've got this heart thing that rules out exercise. This time of year's when all the heavy lifting happens... it's pissing me off," he laughed.

"I bet. I hate slowing down for anything."

A somewhat familiar voice filtered through the fence gate before Noah stepped through. "Hey, babe. Oh – hello!"

Noah had directed the same art show where they'd all met. He was a bit too... well... flamboyant for Chase's taste. Chase respected his artistic vision. It was just hard to be around him for too long.

"Hi," Chase answered with an awkward little wave. "How's it going?"

"Oh, good, can't complain. Well, I *can*, but... nobody will listen," Noah lamented, glancing at Cameron.

"Nope. He just wrapped one art show but he's already taken on two *more*... After complaining all summer about all the work they are." Cameron rolled his eyes.

"I couldn't turn them down." Noah leaned in to kiss Cameron's cheek. He nodded at Jackson as he emerged carrying a plate of burgers.

Chase smiled. "Where?"

"One's a private show by this rich art collector out in Oromocto. The other's at the arts center downtown. I mean, it's a nonprofit... hence, I can't say no. And the first one pays well."

"It's all about money," Chase chuckled. "I mean, yeah, sure, we love art... but..."

Noah half-smiled. "You can't eat art."

"Well, if it's mine, you *could*--" Chase broke off, realizing that was a bit of a morbid joke.

"Oh, Jesus!" Cameron laughed from behind Noah,

handing corn cobs to Jackson to throw on the grill. "No cannibalism jokes before supper."

Noah looked horrified, but he relaxed into a smile. There was a weird pause. Chase couldn't think of anything to say, and apparently, neither could Noah.

Chase moved toward Jackson instead. "Must have been a good summer for barbecuing." It had been hot and dry.

"Perfect. When the sun's starting to go down a little, early evening, it cools off. Now we've got those gates in, it helps. There's less running into and out of houses."

Cameron laughed. "Though certain people kicked out the boards in the fence before we were even moved in."

"Liar. All the boxes were inside, ergo, we were moved in." That was someone Chase didn't recognize. He might have seen him at the show, but he couldn't remember talking to him. He looked a lot like Cameron and Jackson in the nose and eyes, but he was built like Chase or Noah – willowy and slender. He didn't dress as femininely as Noah, though.

It was hard to do anything as femininely as Noah.

"That's our brother Thomas," Jackson added, waving the flipper at him. That easy way of being around each other made Chase's chest ache with yearning.

He wouldn't mind having a family like this.

"Hi," Chase greeted, and Thomas nodded in return. "What's up?"

"Oh, long day at the bank, but I can't complain. Someone came in looking for a savings account we've never offered. We're still not sure where they heard about it from..."

Jackson laughed. "Drama, then."

"For Fredericton, that's drama," Thomas laughed. "And I feel about ten times less likely to get shot here... I used to work in Halifax," he added in explanation for Chase.

Chase nodded. "I've heard about it."

"Grab a plate. Corn's up, guys."

Even though he'd met Noah before the rest of them, Chase still wasn't sure how to react when Noah pirouetted out of Jackson's way and everyone grinned. Something prickled deep inside: resentment, maybe? That was kinda weird.

Chase tried to put it aside and relax with the rest of Jackson's family. Even if it was a painful reminder of what he'd lost, he refused to think directly about *that*.

Chase was going to fucking have fun, and make friends he didn't fuck. He deserved that much.

You can't have this one. Just learn to be okay with that. Didn't stop him from fantasizing a little about what it would be like to kiss Jackson, though.

CHAPTER
Five

THOMAS

AFTER THE BARBECUE, CAMERON HEADED TO NOAH'S PLACE and Jackson started work at his forge. Thomas cleaned his kitchen and made his grocery list while he had a moment to breathe. He left the window open to smell the wood smoke from Jackson's forge.

Neither of them had someone else to cook for, so sometimes they cooked supper together when Cam wasn't around. Jackson tended to go for easy meals when others weren't there. Thomas, however, didn't mind cooking for himself. Even at the end of a long week, it was a nice break. He liked taking that time.

Thomas smiled as he glanced out across their yards from the kitchen window, washing the last few pots. Cam was lucky that he'd met Noah before even properly moving to the city. Thomas had moved back here at the same time in May and Jackson had always lived here.

It's not like I don't try, though.

With that in mind, Thomas dried off his hands and grabbed his laptop. Curled on the sectional couch, he first checked his dating site messages, then browsed for local matches. He was used to seeing the same few faces, but it was possible someone new had signed up.

There was a new match, and his photo looked weirdly familiar.

"Oh, Jesus."

Jackson's Facebook profile photo for ages had been him in front of the walking bridge in town. Before that, he'd had a handsome professional shot taken of him while forging. Those two thumbnails showed up when Thomas hovered over his profile.

His brother was on the dating site, too?

Fuck. Has he already seen me?

Thomas's hand almost shook. He navigated quickly to his recent visitors and scanned the list.

Nope. He'd found Jackson first.

He clicked back to the profile and blocked it before his nerves calmed. It wasn't like it would be *awful* if Jackson figured out he was on the dating site looking for men, but...

It was complicated and Thomas didn't want to get into thinking about it. His two gay brothers of all people would be cool with it, but *he* didn't want to talk to *them*. And for their part, neither of them had ever bugged him, thank god.

He was curious, though. He hadn't heard Jackson mention online dating before. Might be worth stopping by for a chat.

Thomas closed his laptop and headed out to the workshop.

The muffled ringing of metal sounded through the door. Thomas padded through the tall grass en route to the converted workshop building where Jackson had installed his forge. It had been hell to get it up to code, but Thomas knew Jackson was prouder of it than his own house now.

Thomas knocked, not that it would have made a difference, and let himself in. He closed the door after himself to keep the sound down.

"Jesus, it's hot in here." Good thing he was just in a t-shirt and light jeans.

"Oh, I know." Jackson was shirtless and red-cheeked. His gaze was utterly focused on the strips of metal he was hammering together. His big brother was ripped, sweat running down his back as his biceps rippled with the effort of joining metal to metal.

Sometimes Thomas felt bad that he didn't work out even a little compared to his brothers. Then, he remembered that he liked pasta and hated lifting weights. If he never landed a man because of it, fine.

Jackson paused to look over at Thomas. "You all right?"

"Oh, yeah," Thomas smiled. "Need any help?"

"Grab those metal bits and clean them up if you wanna help," Jackson nodded. Thomas went over to start gathering them into a bucket. "Having an exciting Friday night?"

"Not as exciting as yours," Thomas laughed. He examined a few cast-off scraps, wondering if they could be turned into art pieces somehow. Some of them were twisted in cool ways. Maybe that was Jackson's plan. "It was cool to meet Chase earlier, though."

"Yeah, we have coffee now and then. He's nice. A little hard to read sometimes, but nice." Jackson frowned at his metal piece. He folded his arms.

"What's up?"

"Whenever I wonder why I don't have a boyfriend, two

seconds later, I geek out over these – no, seriously, look at these joins. C'mere. Look."

Thomas glanced over at where Jackson pointed. "Well done." Thomas didn't know what he was looking for. It was definitely a section of Cameron's railings for the landing above his living room. It looked... well, just like the plan had shown. "You'll find a man who appreciates... well-forged joins."

Jackson laughed and turned the whole metal piece over. It clanged against the table as he inspected the cooling rods he'd just joined. "Thanks for your vote of confidence."

"Have you thought about trying?" Thomas asked casually, hoping he didn't give himself away with some nervous tic.

"Yeah, actually," Jackson answered. He paused and looked at Thomas, but he didn't seem to suspect anything. Instead, he looked back at his piece. "Can you... not tell Cam this?"

Thomas perked up with curiosity. "Of course."

"I just registered for an online dating site. I was getting Chase to help me with my profile." Jackson fidgeted with his hammer, tapping it against the metal here and there.

"Cool," Thomas answered to show his brother that he was fine with it. Jackson *was* a little old-fashioned in some ways.

"Really?"

"Yeah!" Thomas laughed. "Everyone's meeting people online these days. But why not tell Cam? He wouldn't mind either."

Jackson rolled his eyes. "Cause he'll make fun of me."

Thomas snorted with laughter. "Oh, can't take the heat?"

"Fuck off and get us a couple beers from my fridge," Jackson laughed.

Thomas grinned and punched Jackson's shoulder on the

way by. "Let me know if you meet up with anyone on there, yeah?"

"I will. Thanks, man." Jackson looked more relaxed already and offered Thomas a smile. Little did Jackson know that Thomas had other reasons for offering brotherly support. Then, the question Thomas was hoping not to hear. "Hey, what about you?"

"What about those beers?" Thomas countered with a grin and walked out to grab them. He knew Jackson would let it drop when he came back to the workshop... Jackson and Cam took hints well.

CHAPTER
Six

JACKSON

After he finally put out the forge for the night, Thomas having long since gone to read, Jackson checked his messages. So far, just a student who was too young for him and two guys who wanted to hook up.

He reminded himself what Chase had said. It would take time before people found his profile, and he should browse profiles and message others. With Thomas's support, he'd have a second opinion if he wasn't sure about someone. Thomas was a scarily accurate judge of character, and he didn't hold back with the truth. At least Thomas rarely made fun of Cam and Jackson like they did each other.

Even though Jackson wanted a date, he just couldn't be bothered to actively look for one.

He rubbed his chin as he set aside his laptop and turned on the television instead.

A date implied romantic pressure. Then there was that awkward chemistry assessment, and the bit where they tried to work out who was a top. Some guys weren't ballsy enough to just ask. Most assumed he was, anyway, and they weren't wrong.

Jackson wished he could have something a bit more... comfortable. Kind of like when Chase hung around, but with chemistry.

Well, with *mutual* chemistry.

Jackson had felt a weird moment when he'd walked Chase to his front door to collect his sweater before seeing him off. It was like the end of a first date when you didn't know whether to go for a hug or a kiss or a handshake. Jackson had ended up offering a handshake and half-hug in thanks for the profile help.

In response, Chase had just given him a polite "bye for now" and smiled. He must not have felt the same potential as Jackson. Jackson's arm had slid around that willowy body for a hug and Chase's warm body had pressed up against his...

He drew a breath and let it out, trying to get those thoughts out of his head.

Fuck. Maybe I do need to get laid if I'm thinking about buddies like that.

Jackson reopened one of the messages, but the gut feeling he had in response made him close it again.

It was worth waiting for more.

CHAPTER
Seven

CHASE

THE MUSIC WAS POUNDING BY THE TIME CHASE MADE IT TO the only gay club in the city. It was clean and classy, with lights and music that always made Chase feel a little higher on life. And the drinks were good and cheap. Even if it had been expensive and overrated, he still would've had to go. It was one of like, *two*, in the whole province.

Ugh, this place sometimes.

But it was so out of the way that it was the last place anyone would think to look for him.

It had been a long night, and still nobody had bitten. "Another cooler, please," he called over the counter to the bartender. He didn't even mind the music being loud up here by the bar. It was okay, sometimes, not to have to make conversation with the guys standing next to him.

After Chase paid for his cooler, he turned and leaned against the counter. Time to scan the room for available men.

It was often the same kind of crowd from week to week, so he already saw at least half a dozen guys he'd gone home with. He chugged from the bottle and decided he wanted someone new, but wouldn't complain if it were a repeat.

The club wasn't just for gay guys. The queers and freaks and shy people who didn't feel comfortable going out to mainstream bars wound up here. Lots of students who were flexible in their gender or sexuality, too. Then there were visitors from small towns looking to join the "big city's" nightlife.

It was a good thing. It made for some variety; otherwise it would have been the same hundred guys all the time.

Chase liked that he got so much attention here. Sure, every pickup line was the same, but it took the effort out of it. He wore his short-sleeved shirt or a low V-neck t-shirt to show off his tattoos. It made it easy for guys to approach and talk to him about them.

Some nights, like tonight, the conversation didn't go anywhere with anyone, though. The club was nearly closing and there still wasn't a nibble. It was frustrating.

He heard someone talking over the music and turned to take him in. "Nice tats."

"Thanks," Chase automatically answered. The guy was a little taller than him, with broad shoulders and blond hair, a wicked smile. He had nice lips, at least. It might have been just the lighting, but his skin looked a little darker... Italian? He had the curly hair for it. "I'm Chase."

"Antonio."

Definitely Italian. Someone foreign – that was a bit more interesting. He turned to face Antonio. "Studying abroad?"

"Yeah. It's my first semester, so I moved here on August first to start my lease." Antonio looked casual. He wore a short-sleeved collared shirt of his own, and nice, smooth-looking trousers. He dressed well. All the Europeans did –

the few who wound up in this city, anyway. Not a lot of people wanted to study abroad here compared to, say, Vancouver or Halifax or Toronto.

Chase nodded, taking a few deep gulps of his cooler. The accented words rolled off Antonio's tongue effortlessly. "You speak good English. Did you grow up speaking it?"

"Yes. English, French, and Italian. They're all pretty easy to learn." Antonio's eyes were raking up and down his body.

"We learn French, too, but it's Québécois. A little more slangy, I hear." Desire burned through Chase's body in response to the look. Just being wanted was enough to make him tingle. Being lusted after was even better.

Being lusted after by a stranger, someone he didn't have to look in the eye later, was fucking perfect.

It was probably sick, but that was the way it was: Chase needed to be wanted by people who didn't know who he was. Once the relationship got deeper, he got scared off. He was used to it and he adapted his dating patterns accordingly.

Antonio chuckled. His eyes were back on Chase's, and there was no doubt what he wanted. He slowly raised his bottle to his lips and tipped it back to drain it. He slid it across the bar and held out his hand. "Shall we dance or go to my car?"

The unspoken message: *Why even bother pretending?*

No need to feign interest when they could cut to the chase.

Chase answered, "You parked nearby?" He gulped the last few sips of his drink and pushed the bottle back, too. He stood up.

"In the library parking lot."

"That's pretty close."

Antonio's hand rested on his back to steer him out of the club. Chase avoided eye contact with the bouncer on the way by. Not that he felt guilty. He was fucking lucky, getting taken home by the hot new foreign exchange student without a fuss.

Chase's nerves tingled with the firm pressure on his back. As they waited for a taxi to pass before jaywalking, Antonio's hand slowly rubbed up his spine. He rubbed all the way up to his shoulder and back down. The slow circles of palm against his skin kept him on edge. Chase couldn't distract himself any longer: his cock started to stiffen.

"Do you like Fredericton?" Antonio chatted, in the tone of a man who was making more or less polite conversation. This was what Chase relished: being touched and desired, sharing bits of their lives without having to commit later. Without risking anything.

"It's not bad. You? So far?"

"I would say the same." Antonio snorted. "I had to buy a car in my first week, though. The buses here are... lame."

Chase laughed. Some slang was easy to pick up.

The walk to Antonio's car was short. That was lucky, since they kept bumping into each other's side deliberately. They touched each other's arm or back, and sometimes outer thighs. Once, Antonio reached in front of Chase to press a crosswalk button even though the street was empty. While pulling his hand back to himself, Antonio groped him.

Chase was aching for him. He strode across the street to wait while Antonio unlocked the car.

"You live nearby?"

"Uptown."

Chase grimaced. That was a long walk home for him.

"There's nobody else around," Antonio observed mildly, watching him with those dark, lustful eyes.

Easy decision. Chase opened the back door and climbed in. It wasn't the first time he'd fucked in a stranger's backseat, and he was sure it wouldn't be the last.

Antonio tumbled on top of him, just barely pulling the door closed behind him. His body already blanketed Chase's. He pushed his knee into the backseat and straddled Chase. As he ground against him, Antonio yanked him up by the shirt to kiss him hard.

Chase moaned into Antonio's mouth. His hard cock appreciated the pressure of a hip – and then another cock pressing forward through layers of fabric.

"You have anything?"

"Huh?" Chase pressed a few more kisses to Antonio's lips.

Antonio gently sucked his lower lip. He whispered, "Tested?"

"Ah. Yeah. Nothing. You?"

"I'm good. And you are very handsome," Antonio whispered. His breath was hot on Chase's lips as they pulled apart. Chase's heart pounded and body burned from the contact. "I spotted you instantly."

Chase's ego soared. He couldn't help a grin. "Yeah? You're pretty hard to miss, too." He reached up to comb a hand back through that thick, curly hair. *Soft* hair, too, Jesus.

That reminded him that he'd meant to check something. Chase reached down to run his hands across Antonio's ass, squeezing. His trousers *did* feel good. Probably some fancy Italian brand.

Antonio moaned, and Chase squeezed again, pulling him in tightly between his legs. He reached between them to fumble and get his jeans down.

When Chase's cock met open air, it throbbed with pleasure. He spread his legs, one knee bumping the back of the driver's seat while the other pressed up against the seat. He licked his own fingers and slid them inside, not wanting to allow Antonio this intimacy.

Antonio seemed fine with it – he was busy getting a condom on anyway. Chase couldn't see a lot of his dick in the dark backseat, but enough of it to know he'd feel it. Phew.

When his fingers slid out of himself, the lubricated condom tip – and he was thankful for that – pressed against him. Chase dug his fingers into his own thigh and he gasped and rolled his head back at the penetration. The window steamed up behind them with the heat of their desire-laden breaths.

Antonio was thin but long, at least, almost filling him. He had a nice curve to him, but not the best Chase had felt.

At least he was good at fucking. The car rocked with the force of Antonio's thrusts inside him. His head rubbed across the prostate to send thrills of arousal through Chase's tense body.

"Gorgeous," Antonio praised. Chase realized it had been a while since a hookup praised him during sex instead of just before it.

"So are you," Chase murmured, and he meant it. Pretty, if not the guy he'd bring home for a date.

Antonio leaned down, pulling his shirt up around his chest so he could kiss along the tattoos over his chest and on his side.

Chase let the little sparks of desire be fanned into flames by the hot, wet pressure against bare skin. Antonio's thrusts grew harder and he was overcome by the moment. All rational thought was swept away by the mindless desire to come and make Antonio come, too.

Their grunts, moans, and the wet sound of sex and kisses echoed in the confines of Antonio's car. When Antonio came a minute or two later, his cock was buried deep in Chase. Chase rolled his head back to expose his throat and groaned. He reached down to stroke himself hard, their bodies still locked together. Antonio thrust with each little quiver of his body and muscles.

It was all sex and no space to breathe, utterly over-whelming Chase. Just the way he liked it.

Chase came hard, gritting his teeth together to try to stifle the sound as he cried out and grunted. He kept his hand over the tip of his cock to catch the mess so he didn't fuck up Antonio's seat. He clenched hard around Antonio's softening cock, his back arching as his chest heaved. He was half-desperate for breath for a few seconds. Once he caught it, he settled back down again.

"Thank you," Antonio murmured. "Very considerate."

Chase laughed breathlessly. The tension drained out of his body and Antonio slipped out. "Anytime. Got a tissue?"

"Here." Antonio pressed one into his hand and he used it to wipe both his hands clean. Antonio had a trash bag under the driver's seat, so Chase put it in there. "Here good?"

"Yes." Antonio added his condom to the bag.

Antonio tried to brace himself above Chase so he could pull his pants back up and button them. Once he was decent, he wiped off both backseat windows. He pushed open the door by their feet and slid backward out of the seat.

That gave Chase enough space to yank his own jeans back up and clean up, tucking his shirt back into his waistband.

Antonio eyed him as he pulled himself out of the car, holding the back door open for him. "Thanks, gorgeous." He leaned in to air-kiss both of Chase's cheeks. It was an awkwardly intimate move compared to the usual rush out the door.

"You, too," Chase answered automatically, puckering his lips but not actually meeting skin. "Good luck in Fredericton."

A whole semester or more of seeing this guy at the club. Oh, well, I'd do him again.

It wasn't a long walk back home from here, but Chase still had a good ten or fifteen minutes to think about the nitty-gritty.

The way Antonio had watched him and told him he was sexy was... well, hotter than he'd had in a while. He hadn't been great on giving Chase pleasure, but a lot of guys didn't do that, either. It had been ages since anyone had even given him head.

Three AM thoughts were *always* destructive. Chase couldn't help them sneaking into his mind, though. He was good to be fucked or lusted after – he knew that much. Anything more? Nah. He wasn't interested anyway.

Chase kept his head down as he padded through the halls to his apartment. Getting exactly what he'd wanted that night didn't stop him feeling the usual low, twisting feeling in his stomach.

If what he wanted wasn't what he needed, what was?

CHAPTER
Eight
JACKSON

JACKSON'S GAZE FOCUSED INTENTLY ON THE FIREPLACE mantel. It had always looked kind of cheap and factory-made, but he'd been willing to deal with it.

Might as well put it on the list.

As he walked around his house, notebook in hand, he wrote down his planned renovations. He wanted to combine the master bedroom with the small bedroom right next door, swap out the fireplace mantel, and rebuild the porch.

Jackson approached the sliding glass doors in the dining room. Another item occurred to him: a stone path out to the forge. It was just grass out to the shed. There was a worn dirt driveway around the side of the building to pull up his truck and load up materials or his work or take deliveries. Between the house and the front door of the workshop, though, there was nothing.

A proper path would be nice, complete with more back-yard landscaping. It would be nice to have a private area near the house if he wanted one while his brothers used the barbecue. He envisioned each of them with a gazebo and privacy screening in a corner of their own yard.

After Jackson wrote that down, his gaze was drawn to the basement stairs. He rarely went down there except to grab things in storage, even though it was a neat little walkout space. Making it into a bachelor zone would be awesome.

The kitchen was fine for his needs and he didn't need spare bedrooms anyway. As a single guy, he didn't have to worry about sharing office space with anyone. He didn't anticipate that changing soon.

Might as well put his real estate to good use for himself.

Once he completed his list, he cut through the backyard to Cameron's place and headed in to join his brother. "Okay, I got the list."

Cameron patted the couch next to him and muted the TV while he grabbed his own notebook. "Right. Whatcha got?"

Jackson read out his list and Cameron nodded after each item. When he was done, Jackson raised his eyes to Cameron's. "Is that asking too much?"

"Nah. It's just gonna take me a little while over the winter to finish everything. Winter isn't the best construction time. I don't think I can get much done before surgery – at least, I can't bank on it."

"Right, no, of course," Jackson agreed. "I was thinking for after you recover, too. We can source materials in the meantime. My basement's almost empty and I can drive up to it from the path out to my workshop, so we can store materials in there."

"Really? Yeah, that's a good idea." Cameron rubbed his chin. "So each of us buys our own materials and then we swap labor until we're both happy with our houses, yeah?"

That sounded fair to Jackson. "Unless you decide you

want a fuckin' mansion worth of work. Then you can pay me."

Cameron laughed. "No mansions," he promised. "What about Thomas?"

"He can help us..." Jackson trailed off, wondering what his little brother felt comfortable doing. He didn't seem to mind tidying up after them, but he was never one to rush to do the heavy lifting and prove himself. Then again, with Jackson and Cam competing a little on that front, he never had to.

"He's good at painting," Cameron continued. "I put him to work when I was doing my construction job. Back when he was in high school, remember? He said he needed the cash and he did it all summer."

"Ohhh, yeah, right." Jackson had forgotten about that summer job. "Well, all three houses do need paint." Then, he paused. "Did we ever find out what that was for?"

"No. For all we know he has some savings account overseas. He's secretly a millionaire now," Cameron laughed.

Jackson grinned. He wouldn't put it past Thomas.

Still, there were moments that made him worry. Sometimes he felt like he knew his little brother very well. Other times he realized he didn't know a lot of things about him.

Thomas steered the conversation away from dating, and he never talked about his future plans. He just skirted away from certain deeper topics, despite being a deep person. It was paradoxical and... well, frustrating.

"He seems happy to be here," Cameron commented, his mind working along the same lines. "He talking to you much?"

"Yeah, now and then he comes to help me in the workshop." *Can't tell him what the last conversation was about.* "Still doesn't really talk much."

"Well, we haven't seen a lot of him since he graduated, and even before then. Especially me," Cameron frowned.

"Hey, not your fault," Jackson reminded Cam. He was as firm as always when his brother felt guilty about his busy past life as a pro hockey player. "Things are changing now."

"Yeah, they are."

Come to think of it, Thomas had never talked to Jackson once about dating before now. Maybe things were changing more than Jackson knew.

CHAPTER
Nine
CHASE

"I don't know, Floyd." Chase leaned on his elbow as he watched his boss and friend rearrange sketchbooks and photo books. He was trying to keep his tone casual. "Someone could still recognize my work."

"Okay, man, I know I said I wouldn't ask..."

Chase straightened up, his heart starting to thump with nerves. The other man was a little heavier-set than him, and had even more tattoos. He had about five years on him, too. Chase could take him. *No, wait, what the fuck? Where did that come from?* The guy wasn't about to leap over the counter at him just because he didn't have an art portfolio.

"You came here saying you'd worked for years but you couldn't use your portfolio online. Now you're telling me you can't even show people a physical copy? I mean, it's not like people can Google image search in real time."

Chase swallowed hard. "No..."

Floyd made eye contact. He pulled up a chair and sat down opposite Chase. "Talk to me, man. We're buddies, right?"

More so than anyone else Chase knew, yeah. "Definitely." Chase was still reluctant. It was like dragging himself across hot coals to think about it, let alone spill his guts to someone else. "It's just... pretty raw."

"Then the shop's closed." Floyd stood up and flipped the sign over. He approached Chase and reached out to touch his arm, leaning on the other side of the counter. He smelled like citrus and sweet things. "Man, you get twitchy when new people walk in. You hate seeing parents bring their kids. You wrap yourself up in your own head even when we're going out for drinks..."

All true.

"Who are you running from? We can get you help."

Chase swallowed hard. He'd been dreading this conversation for months. Everyone always figured out that something was up, and then there'd be pity. At least he knew it wasn't a pity friendship – Floyd had been straight with him from the beginning.

The easiest way to put it was also the simplest. "My family... didn't take me coming out very well."

Floyd's face fell and his brows furrowed in anger. "I'm sorry. Are you safe here?"

"I don't... I don't know. I think so."

"You don't feel safe, though, huh?" Floyd had a knowing look, but there was something else about him. "Little bit of advice... Find something that makes you feel stronger. Kickboxing or archery or wrestling or... whatever floats your boat."

Floyd did competitive archery, and for the first time, Chase wondered why. He lifted his head to watch his friend instead of shying away from eye contact. Floyd knew a lot more about what his mental state was like than he was letting on.

"It's just... on top of everything else," Chase sighed. "It's hard living here. And I don't know what I want in a relationship. And everything else is rocky at the same time. All of it together, I guess, is the problem." It was a little painful being forced to talk about this, but Floyd wasn't letting him get away.

"Yeah. Then finding that one good thing can help stabilize the rest of it."

Maybe Floyd was right. It *sounded* like it made sense, at least.

When he didn't shoot down the idea, Floyd continued. "You're being a hermit. You spend all your time working here and making money or fucking the night away at the club. Not... you know, knowing people. You're not even on Facebook."

Chase's stomach twisted with anxiety. "People could find me there."

"Exactly. So you gotta get out a little in real life, get some real social supports. That guy you hung out with the other day, the one with the artistic family – talk to him. Meet up with guys for fun or hanging out, not just jumping into bed."

Floyd slept around, too, but to be fair... Floyd seemed a lot happier about it than Chase felt. Or maybe he felt that gnawing pit in his stomach at the end of a night out, too, and he just didn't admit it.

Chase nodded. "Yeah," he murmured. "Yeah, I'll look up some things."

"I'll drive you to your first meeting of whatever it is. University's back, so check out the clubs there, too. Some of them take non-students."

"You're determined to see me make friends," Chase laughed. Floyd had been bugging him for months to get out there, but he'd never followed through like now. It was... It was nice to have someone care that much about him, though.

Floyd nodded. "Yeah. We all need 'em." He clapped Chase's back, then leaned in for a brief, manly hug.

Chase clapped Floyd's back, his mind already wandering over the possibilities. Archery sounded kinda fun. For the only other guy here, apart from Jackson, who hadn't yet taken him home, Floyd was pretty cool.

"This is going to be the most awkward part of tonight. Fencing isn't just about attacking. It's about maintaining your own personal space, and being aware of it."

Chase grimaced.

"Look at you all. You're not going to die from holding hands a little."

That produced a laugh from the class of a dozen or so fencing newbies who had shown up to the first session of this course. There were three lessons a week, an intense pace. Chase had barely squeaked in to take the last available spot in the course. It had started the day after his conversation with Floyd.

Pair by pair, they reached out to entwine their fingers with each other's. There was awkward, nervous chuckling from the pairs of men. Chase rolled his eyes and ignored it, focusing on his partner's personal space.

They walked toward each other, bending their arms slowly. They got accustomed to how far away they were when their elbows bent.

Already, Chase could see a sword keeping everyone out of his personal space bubble. That was apparently going to be the point of the next lesson.

Although the first lesson was mostly history that he tuned out, however hard he tried to listen, these few exercises were interesting. They played soccer with tennis balls, and then started to learn footwork. They tried to keep the tennis balls between their feet in one exercise. In another, they passed balls back and forth to each other as they stepped back and forth.

By the time the lesson was over, he found himself more excited for the next lesson than he'd anticipated.

A few of the students stayed behind to ask questions: what kind of swords they'd use, how long it took to learn, and where to buy swords. *That* was what Chase wanted to know. The instructor said the club had some practice gear to provide and then rent after the course was done. Those who liked the aesthetic of weapons were welcome to buy them, but almost all weren't competition-legal.

Chase didn't care. The idea of having a blade in his house made him feel safer. He didn't really care about competition. He just wanted to be able to keep people out of his space.

He smiled as he headed out onto the street, noting how far away objects he passed were – telephone posts, street signs, even parked cars. *In my bubble – outside of my bubble – oh, that one's inside my bubble...*

He'd never had the best sense of spatial dimensions aside from micro-scale proportions on people's bodies. People often startled him by getting close before he even knew it, and it always made his heart leap into his throat. Tonight, he didn't feel anxious walking through the downtown bustle and back to his apartment building.

Something subtle had changed within him at class that evening.

CHAPTER
Ten

JACKSON

"Look at how far along I am," Jackson grinned. He lowered the heavy wrought iron piece to rest against Cam's living room carpet.

"Oh wow, that whole section is complete, isn't it? It looks finished..."

"Yeah, it's done. That's the whole section between those staircase landings," Jackson told him. "Then I just have to do the section along the top. You like it?"

"What does it look like in place?"

Jackson laughed. "You're just making me work for it, aren't you?" He hauled it up a few steps and over the edge of the bannister. "Now, imagine that the other crappy railings aren't there..."

"Oh, no, I see what you mean. Wow. That'll look stunning," Cam told him sincerely. "Thank you, bro. That's... really cool."

Jackson's chest swelled. He carried the section back downstairs and leaned it behind the couch with the other two. "No problem."

"Will it fit the code?"

"Building code? I already measured like eight times, man."

Cameron frowned. "But it will?"

Jackson groaned. "Yes. I know the codes, man."

"I'm just saying, this is a big custom piece. No builder involved to get the permits and stuff like usual..."

"You're a stickler for the rules, aren't you?" Jackson's temper was heating up, but he tried to take a breath and cool it off.

"Do I need to hire a lead contractor here to keep you in line?" Cam smirked. There was an edge of tension between them that Jackson didn't like. Cam was worried he'd fuck up the spacing between the stairs and open air and fail inspection.

Jackson punched Cameron's arm a little harder than usual. "I'm not gonna fuck up. I've been working with carpenters and inspectors longer than you *were* a carpenter – for what, one summer?"

Cameron's cheeks flushed red and he took the point. "Yeah. Sorry."

"Yeah." Jackson rubbed his chin. "Okay, I gotta blow this popsicle stand. See you later, man."

"You too."

Once he was in the backyard, Jackson scowled at the gate as he stepped through it and slid it shut. His little brother usually believed in him, but now he was suddenly questioning him?

Jackson knew it was just Cam being cautious, but it still rankled. If only he *didn't* know the code by heart. He wished he could work mostly on art or armor or fireplace accessories. He didn't love railings and balusters. But the home builders were expanding suburbs rapidly. They built new subdivisions every year. Their jobs were the most consistent and straightforward... and they paid well.

They just bored the crap out of him.

He knew when he started to get annoyed easily it was time to step back from work. He went to his forge to shut everything down. Ryan and Kevin and the guys were all busy and he hadn't heard from Chase since they'd set up his dating profile. He sent a text.

Wanna hang out?

He didn't know why his heart thumped as he waited for a response.

CHAPTER
Eleven

CHASE

"EN GARDE."

Chase's hand almost shook, even though the flexible sword in his hand was surprisingly light. It wasn't even as heavy as his tattoo gun. The tip was covered in a bright orange cover, yet it felt... far more deadly.

His opponent, Belle, was clad in a mask and heavy clothing. She looked far more intimidating than he'd expected. He swallowed hard, trying to keep his feet pointed like he'd been taught. He imagined the tennis ball between them. Seconds later, that was forgotten. Belle lunged forward and he hastily brought his blade across to parry the blow.

Every second felt like years when he was waiting for the next blow.

Twice more his opponent tried before he got up the courage to lunge, too. Belle had fenced before, and it showed in the smooth way she moved.

"That's it, Chase," their teacher, Mike, called out. "Keep going."

Belle lunged again. This time, he noticed the moment the

lightweight foil entered his personal space. The moment he'd parried her blow, he countered and the orange tip pressed against her chest plate.

"Whoa, good," she praised, and her voice sounded surprised but pleased for him.

Mike echoed, "Good. Both of you stand down. You two, you're next."

As they rotated off and set down their foils, Belle lifted her mask and smiled at Chase as soon as his was off. "That was great."

Chase was still shaking. His adrenaline was through the roof. His thick protective equipment weighed him down and grounded him at least. "Thanks."

"You go to school here?"

"No, but I just moved here a few months ago."

Belle smiled, tucking her hair behind her ear. "Cool. I can't believe this is only the third lesson. I've learned a lot."

"Really? You seemed pretty good already."

"Oh, no, I forgot most of what I learned before," Belle laughed. "But it does come more naturally to you after lessons, I guess. You're coming along fast too."

"Thanks."

They turned their attention back to the current pair to try and study them. Chase smiled as he leaned back against the wall. Maybe he could pick up a couple friends here, too.

By the time the session was done, Chase was ready to go, though. When he got a text message from Jackson asking him to hang out, he stopped mid-walk to Tim Horton's to answer.

Sure :) I was just about to grab supper.

Let's meet up for supper? Jackson answered.

"Yes," Chase whispered under his breath and answered,

Sure! It would give him the chance to propose a crazy little idea. He told himself that was the only reason he was excited. Something about the way his heart warmed up said otherwise.

Jackson was dressed up nicely and waiting at the door to the restaurant. Chase's heart unexpectedly fluttered. It had been a long time since his last date.

Not that he wanted one with Jackson.

Chase cleared his throat and raised a hand to wave. He tried not to notice Jackson's clean, dark jeans, freshly-styled hair, or the ironed collared shirt. This was a step up from the usual t-shirt and jeans.

"Hey," Jackson smiled, and for a moment, there was that hesitation again. *Just like when he saw me off last time.*

Chase broke the tension by smiling and clapping Jackson's arm. He pulled open the door for them both. If Jackson didn't want things to be romantic between them, he wouldn't make this awkward. "How's it going?"

Jackson relaxed and offered him a smile. "Thanks. Not bad, just finished up some work for my brother. It's nice getting to swap work, even if it's a bit more of the same. Table for two, please."

Once they were seated, Chase leaned in across the table and folded his arms. "More of the same?"

"Always staircases," Jackson groaned. "I'm getting tired of them. I just want to make, I don't know... armor."

Chase's cheeks turned pink. This was going to sound so cheeky, but... "Well, I have an idea. Um, I kind of want... a sword..."

"Yeah?" Jackson clearly saw where this was going.

"We could trade, somehow... if you're interested. I mean, back when we met, you said you were thinking of getting a secret tattoo. I don't know if you did that yet--" Jackson shook his head, so Chase continued, "--but I could help."

"In exchange for a sword? What kind? I can't do copyrighted stuff," Jackson told him upfront. "And I can't do something you can actually fight with – at least, it'd take me a long time."

Chase blinked and laughed. "No, I'm not going for Lord of the Rings-style swords," he reassured Jackson.

"You'd be surprised how many guys want to pretend they're in it," Jackson grinned.

Their waiter took their drink orders. Jackson and Chase quickly picked their meals to order at the same time.

Once the waiter left, Chase looked back at Jackson. "But, no, kind of the style of an old-fashioned fencing sword, I guess?"

"Ahh. Foil? Sabre? I can't do everything," Jackson warned.

"I don't have a particular style in mind. I know it's not competition-legal."

"I can't do those either."

"Right, right. I just want something to... I don't know, make me feel a bit safer. If I can bring it to some medieval festival someday, so much the better. But something I can display and... know I have around."

Jackson looked at him oddly for a moment before he nodded. "Well, I want a family tattoo done."

Aww, he's sweet. I hope he doesn't regret that, though. "Oh, family tattoos aren't always a good idea," Chase laughed under his breath. "So many people wind up getting laser removal when they have family fights."

"I'm not fuckin' doing that," Jackson answered, his voice much sharper than Chase expected.

Chase flinched hard.

Instantly, Jackson frowned an apology. He reached out with an open hand across the table to touch his arm. When he touched him, Chase's nerves crackled with pleasure. "Sorry, man. No, I didn't mean that at you."

"No, sorry," Cameron murmured. "I hit a nerve...?"

Jackson hesitated before he nodded. "I want it as a family thing... before my brother's heart surgery."

Now Chase felt like crap. His eyes widened. "Is it Cam?"

"Yep."

Chase winced. No matter how he felt about family, he ached for Jackson. He could see why Jackson was touchy. "Shit. I'm sorry. That has to be stressful."

"It... It hasn't been easy." Jackson looked a little more raw than Chase had seen him – like he'd looked when he talked about online dating. "It's called CPVT, have you heard of it?" Chase shook his head. "Well, it's a bit rarer. They took months to diagnose it because it usually shows up way earlier. I mean, occasionally you get older people diagnosed. Apparently it's usually *after* they go into cardiac arrest. In the States, I'm sure they would've diagnosed it in days. But because the public health system in Canada is--"

"--shit," Chase chimed in, nodding his agreement. "Oh yeah."

"It took a really good specialist and he had to go back to Ontario in July, middle of his work season..."

Jackson's passion about his brother made Chase smile with familiarity. If any doctor tried to fuck over his little brother... but he didn't have a say in that anymore. *Not the moment. This is about Jackson, not me.*

Jackson cut himself off, then cleared his throat. "Anyway, they know what he needs now. They think it won't have a lot of risk, but... he kinda doesn't have a choice."

The waiter came back with their drinks. Chase took a good few gulps of beer to wash out the bitter taste of regret for his ill-timed joke. Then, he leaned forward again. "Sorry I said that."

Jackson seemed to have to think for a moment to remember. "What? Oh, no, I shouldn't have snapped. I get a little defensive about the people I care about. But you're right, overall. Like, boyfriends' names and stuff are stupid."

Chase laughed at the honesty. "Well... yeah, I think so, but I'll do them if they've been together for decades or something. That's different."

"You can know you want to spend your life with someone in weeks, though."

It was Chase's turn to feel hot under the collar. He tugged it a little as he sipped his beer, then shook his head. "You can *think* you know them."

"But if you both have the same approach to a relationship..."

"Like knowing that they told you the truth about themselves? What if they were lying?" This wasn't even an argument, oddly enough. Chase hadn't had a passionate discussion that wasn't a shouting fight in forever.

Jackson was sitting up straight, too. He looked much less stressed and livelier now. "Well, if they weren't deceiving you about the kind of person they are. I mean, if they clearly want to work to grow the relationship and be honest from the start..."

"Well, yeah, but they could just be... I don't know, tricking you."

Jackson furrowed his brow. "How? By saying they want to be real and then... not being real?"

"Yeah, exactly."

Jackson hummed and leaned back in his chair. His lips pursed, and Chase watched them without meaning to. "Yeah, I see your point. But – I dunno. I like to give people the benefit of the doubt."

He was sweet all over. Chase just hoped not too many guys would take advantage of him while he was dating. Speaking of which...

"Have you met anyone from online?"

"Nah, not yet," Jackson shook his head. "I haven't been looking. I don't know, I just think it's weird. Like, how would I know if I'm going to click with someone and have conversations like this on our first date or not?"

Chase felt heat flush to his cheeks. *He* was being used as an example of someone who clicked with Jackson? Something about that made his heart flutter in a familiar way that he hadn't felt in a long time. Was it possible Jackson thought he was hot, too?

No way... He's always been a gentleman. Wait. Unless that's just the way he is...

Chase leaned forward a little, but he didn't have the balls to follow through on the response he wanted to give. Instead, he answered, "You try it out just to see."

I... I wouldn't mind trying him *out. Just to see.*

Chase drained the rest of his beer, his gaze sliding to their food order that was now arriving. That made for an easy subject change, at least.

They lapsed into comfortable conversation for dinner. Jackson agreed to come over tomorrow evening after the tattoo shop closed. They'd talk then about the services they wanted to trade.

Chase couldn't get that sudden thought out of his mind the whole time, even as he waved goodbye.

Why was Jackson suddenly catching his eye in a way he hadn't thought possible? He *had* to stop thinking about his friends like this.

CHAPTER
Twelve

JACKSON

"Hey, Chase. How's it goin'?"

Was that too casual? Or too flirty? Was he too early? Jackson tried to stop his mind from wandering and worrying over what he was doing seeing Chase again so soon. He was definitely *not* interested in Chase, right? Not if Chase wasn't interested in him...

The way Chase smiled at him in greeting made him wonder. His body warmed up as Chase's brown eyes lit up at the sight of him. Chase unfolded his arms and straightened up from where he leaned against the counter. "Hi! Good, you?" His smile was so cute.

"Great, thanks. This too early?"

"No, no. It's usually slow for the last bit. People don't come in to get work done *right* before closing. Just to book appointments, if that."

Jackson nodded and approached the counter, setting his sketchbook down on it. "So, ready to go over what we're looking for?"

"Yeah. Hold on, let me grab my book." Chase stepped into

the back office. In the meantime, Jackson flipped through the photo albums on the counter.

One was labeled *Floyd* and one *Teri*, but there wasn't one for Chase. Were these the tattooists? When Chase returned, Jackson pointed them out. "None for you?"

Chase's eyes flickered up to Jackson's, his shoulders rising. The defensive moment was gone as fast as that before he pointed to his arms. "There's my portfolio."

Jackson laughed. "I bet you use that line a lot."

"I do, yeah," Chase joined in the laugh. He came around the counter to stand next to Jackson, flipping his own sketchbook open.

"Can I check them out?"

"Oh, yeah, of course." Chase leaned his hip on the counter and offered his arm, turning it this way and that. Jackson sidled closer, trying not to brush too close to him.

A lion stood proud on one arm, its every contour rippling with majesty. It blended into a rippling series of dusky blue and lavender clouds, then pale red roses. Further down, toward Chase's wrist, thorny green branches were entwined with the roses.

On Chase's other arm, a peacock spread its wings in flight. The tail feathers wrapped intricately around his elbow all the way down to his wrist. The same dusky blue and lavender clouds set it off in the background.

Just as when they'd first met, Jackson marveled over the smooth swirls of that style. "Wow," Jackson murmured. "That's... that's really detailed. Did you do all this?"

"I had to get some people to help me fill in a few bits and hold mirrors and stuff. Some spots were an ordeal," Chase laughed. "But most of it."

"I'd like that kind of style on mine, and those kinds of colors."

"All right. Well, we'll talk about it," Chase agreed. "Do you have any concepts?"

Jackson shook his head. "Just some rough ideas." He flipped through his book in search of them. It was always risky to flip through a sketchbook, though. He tried to flip past certain pages quickly.

"Okay, I usually don't comment, but..." Chase spoke up, his tone teasing. "I'll show you mine if you show me yours. If they're not people you know..."

Oh man, he thinks I draw French boys. Jackson blushed. "They're not specific people." He flipped back to his nude sketches. There weren't many – he didn't really draw people aside from modeling his rare human sculptures. He liked to find organic shapes for metal sometimes, though...

"Not bad," Chase murmured, leaning in for a better look at a drawing of a naked man stretched out on his side along the floor. "Did you study drawing people?"

"No, not beyond a basic sketching class."

"That's pretty good."

Jackson smiled at the compliment. It wasn't over-the-top, but it was sincere praise. "Thank you. What about you?"

Chase had been waiting for him to ask. He beamed and flipped open his notebook, turning back a good chunk of pages.

Oh, shit. His men were *hunks.* They were all strong and posed in masculine ways – one from the side, looking sideways and flexing an arm. Another was from behind, the man's head rolled back and arms spread. A third showed him from the front, curling a strong bicep across his muscled chest.

"Wow," Jackson grinned, his gaze returning to his own page. He'd drawn willowy men with strong cheekbones, keen eyes, and a little light muscle. His men actually looked a little like Chase... And Chase had drawn men like him.

Chase had reached the same conclusion at the same moment. His lips parted as he gazed at Jackson's sketch, then at Jackson and his own notebook.

He was flustered. Jackson had never seen him flustered before. Red crept up his angular cheeks, his pretty pink lips looking...

Oh, no. Jackson wanted to kiss him.

"That based on anyone in particular?" Jackson asked. He hoped his voice didn't sound strained.

"My ex," Chase snorted with laughter. "But he was an asshole, so I don't mind you looking. It's not an exact drawing anyway."

Jackson was startled into a laugh. "Oh. He looks tough."

Chase's smile faded as he looked down at the page. He flipped forward to a blank one again. "Yeah. He was."

Jackson didn't like the way he was shutting down. He was starting to get a horrible sneaking suspicion that this guy had been bad news.

Not again. His little brother Cam had split up from his ex for the umpteenth time earlier that summer, just before meeting Noah. Jackson had talked Cam into blocking that asshole's number at last. Not that he was worried now; Cam was utterly smitten with Noah.

But Jackson knew how to handle this: with a light touch. He let the subject drop and instead teased, "Nice buff men."

Chase looked up, smiling. "Thanks," he laughed. "You can tell my type of man, huh? Yours are a lot more... willowy."

"They are," Jackson agreed, and pulled back from Chase

enough to look him up and down. He winked. "More like you, but not as handsome."

Chase's pink blush deepened to a dark red. His cheeks rounded in pleasure that he was trying not to show. Instead, he stuttered, "S-So, did you have any, uh, ideas for your tattoo?"

That's adorable. Jackson grinned at his sudden bashful behavior. "A few. There's a coat of arms for the Riley family, since we're all from Ireland and northern England."

"Oh, the old shield on your arm kinda thing?"

"Not exactly." Jackson grinned. "Um, ours involves a severed hand dripping blood, held up by two pissed-off lions..."

Chase's eyebrows shot up and he laughed. "Oh, you don't want something really morbid? I mean, I can do bones poking out—"

"*No,*" Jackson spoke over him, pushing Chase away from him lightly. "Ugh, no, that's *not* my style."

"I didn't think so," Chase laughed louder, elbowing him back playfully. Their shoulders brushed and Chase shivered as he leaned in across his sketchbook, uncapping his pen with his lips.

Jackson stared at the red lips wrapped around the smooth plastic pen cap. He imagined them elsewhere for a moment. He quickly looked at Chase's eyes when Chase prompted, "So, the lions?"

"Yeah. The colors are green and gold, maybe yellow."

"Green and yellow lions?"

He was already drawing in quick, confident strokes, outlining a lion from the side just as they appeared on so many family crests. How many had he tattooed already? Or did he just draw from memory? God, he was good. Jackson was a bit jealous.

"It doesn't have to be exactly that," Jackson told him. "That's just one... source of inspiration. I mean, a realistic lion like you've got on your shoulder would be epic. Or there's inside family jokes I could get done."

Chase hummed, eying the lion for a moment. Then, he nodded and straightened up. "How about I doodle a few ideas and show them to you soon? Text me with any suggestions to add to the design or consider. Family jokes or names or anything."

Jackson gave him a grateful smile. "Thanks. I'm pretty open to ideas. I wouldn't mind having something... weapon-y, or otherwise blacksmith-y." Jackson became aware that he was still leaning sideways against the counter facing Chase. They were just a little closer than friends usually stood, and Jackson's heart raced.

Chase raised an eyebrow, leaning in a little further still. "Blacksmith-y? Is that a word?" he teased. His dark eyes fell to Jackson's lips before he dragged his gaze back up to Jackson's eyes again.

He's flirting, too...! Jackson bit back his moment of excitement. He licked his lips and nodding. "It is now. Uh, speaking of which..."

It was his turn to pull back a little so he could flip through his book. He had photos added to the book with little corner squares near his concept sketches.

When he found some swords, he showed Chase. "These are a few that I did last year for one collector... and around here, I have another one... ah, here. I should have brought my portfolio book. That's back at the workshop."

"Hm," Chase rubbed his chin, leaning in across Jackson.

He smelled like leather and hand sanitizer and something fresh and spicy...

A chill ran down Jackson's spine. He tried to lean sideways and watch Chase trace the pattern along the hilt with a finger. He tried *not* to look at the short hair at the back of Chase's neck that he ached to feel against his lips.

Shit. I want him.

"I like that, I think. But I'd like to see other examples."

"Wanna come back to my workshop?" Jackson offered as casually as he could.

He didn't miss the way Chase licked his lips and nipped the lower lip. "Yeah, sure. The shop's just about closed now. You'll just have to wait for me to close up."

"Fine with me," Jackson assured him. "I'll wait outside and be your burly security guy," he added, winking again.

"Oh, my hero." Chase grinned, returning to sketching a few more lions – the heads, the full bodies curled up, one holding a sword... oh, that just looked dumb.

Jackson snickered under his breath.

"Yeah, I didn't expect you to take to that one," Chase grinned. "Sword-fighting lions? No?" He added a second lion, lying on the ground, and drops spurting out of the second lion's chest...

"No!" Jackson laughed and shoved Chase, making him streak the paper with his pen tip. "No, that's horrible!"

Chase laughed richly. He capped his pen and tucked it into his pocket. "Go wait outside. I'll be there in a couple minutes."

Jackson grinned, brushing his hand down Chase's arm from his shoulder to his elbow. He grabbed his sketchbook. "Yes, sir," he teased. The door rattled shut behind him as he stepped out into the mild August evening.

Jackson drew a deep breath to try and calm himself.

He'd made Chase get flustered, but something about Chase was getting to him, too. Was this just because they were both single and around each other? But... no, it wasn't just that.

The conversation last night at the restaurant had shown him a new passion. Chase had only ever been calm and collected around Jackson before. That spark of fiery attitude had made Jackson stop and pay attention.

For some reason, Jackson was even enchanted with Chase's morbid sense of humor. He knew Chase only did it because it got to him, but somehow that made him grin even more to himself. It was like buddies messing around with each other, but... there was more. Especially every time they brushed together.

Something told him it was going to be hot at the forge, and he couldn't wait.

CHAPTER
Thirteen
CHASE

CHASE WAS FUCKED.

He'd found it hard enough to resist flirting with Jackson *before* the gorgeous, intense, sweet man started to flirt with him. Now, it was damn near impossible. Hypersexual was a good description for Chase, but he hadn't cared before.

The one problem? Jackson had said in his dating profile that he wanted a relationship. Chase didn't do relationships.

Chase drummed his fingers on his sketchbook as they walked from the locked-up tattoo shop to Jackson's house. After the initial few moments of awkward silence, Jackson started to chat about tattoos he'd seen on people. Chase took the chance to describe a few common styles and locations.

It was comfortable enough, but there was much more tension in the air. When they looked at each other or their hands bumped, a jolt ran down Chase's spine. He could see Jackson's breath catch, too.

They reached Jackson's house within minutes. Chase hung back to flip through Jackson's portfolio while Jackson lit the forge.

"I'll show you a few common patterns and ways of manipulating the metal." Jackson crouched in front of the box, watching the flames. "We'll see if we can find something you like. I have some ideas..."

"How long have you done this?"

"Oh, a decade. I started at seventeen."

He's twenty-seven? Damn, no wonder he's in such good shape. He's in the prime of his life. Chase watched with mixed arousal and fascination as Jackson chose a metal rod. He heated it, cut it in two, and twisted it to form a hilt-like shape before holding it back in the flames by a pair of huge tongs.

"I'm twenty-five," Chase told him. "I've only been tattooing since I was twenty-one, though. Well, I started at eighteen, but I got licensed at twenty-one."

"Four years' experience is still a long time if you're a good artist. Like you are." Jackson kept his grip firm on the tongs as he turned with the glowing hot metal. He dipped one end in water and screwed that end into a clamp. "So, I'm assuming this sword is for show rather than use. At least, I hope so. I do swords for medieval re-enactors, of which you'll find a lot in your fencing group."

Chase shivered. "Ohh. Yeah, I'm not gonna stab people," he promised. "I just want to... I don't know, feel more secure. I still wouldn't use it unless we're talking a life or death home invader situation."

Jackson nodded. "All right. But you're not planning on swordplay in combat at reenactments?"

"No. Not at all." Chase almost laughed at the idea of him trying to reenact anything from history. It just didn't interest him.

"Then I can make the hilt beautiful and only a bit functional." He was twisting with his tongs, bending the metal around freehand. He made small, controlled movements until it swooped up, looped around, and came back down again. Then, four sharp twists around the center. "The blade would be here... you can come closer."

The glowing metal was terrifying to watch even from the other end of the workshop. Chase swallowed hard and stood up, watching Jackson's expression soften with amusement. He jutted his chin out in response and walked around the table toward the clamped metal.

"That's it," Jackson encouraged. "I won't let it drop on you," he winked, stepping back and shaking off his gloves. He unbuttoned his collared plaid shirt to reveal his usual gray t-shirt and Chase resisted the urge to laugh. It was a bit like a Superman moment. *Supersmith, maybe.*

Chase forgot about the glowing hot metal between them. Jackson's pecs rippled beneath clingy fabric. Chase itched to grab that shirt and pull it up for a better look. "Nice."

Jackson laughed and Chase smirked. He looked back at the metal. "You're good at twisting rods." *I wish I could say I hadn't meant that...* He licked his lips.

"I've had a lot of practice," Jackson answered in a low, smooth voice. He slipped those firm, callused hands back into his leather gloves before picking up his tongs. Once he unclamped the metal, he brought it back to the forge, sliding the rod into the flames. "I haven't made a sword in a while. I might be out of practice."

"If it takes you longer, it takes you longer," Chase murmured. "I'm patient. It'll take me a while to come up with your design, too."

Wood smoke was all he could smell, the hissing and crackling of the forge all he could hear. The tension crackled between them.

Then, Jackson turned, the metal clamped in his hand again, and dipped the end in water. He didn't even flinch as the water sizzled and hissed just under his hands.

Chase was starting to get uncomfortably aroused. Jackson screwed the metal into a clamp again, grabbing tongs and beginning to twist.

White-hot metal gave way like butter. Somehow Jackson's twists were precise enough or the metal cool enough that the metal didn't give way. It twisted perfectly, spirals appearing in the metal like they'd been etched there. "Oh, wow," Chase breathed out.

Jackson grinned. "I like that reaction. I thought I'd go for something elegant and flowing. Match your tattoos."

Chase ran a hand down his arm absently, over where he knew the lion was. He'd admired the curves and swoops in the design of the hockey player statue Jackson had done for the art show where they'd met. Seeing him make those curves in real life, albeit on a much smaller scale, was almost surreal.

Jackson didn't hesitate to grab his hammer or tongs. He reshaped bits of metal with smooth, controlled movements and intently focused eyes.

He focused completely on his work, his stance at the ready. His biceps flexed with the weight of the hammer in his hand... Sweat trickled down his back, gleaming on his forehead.

Chase could only imagine Jackson's bare body on the sheets, making love on a hot summer night.

He was half-hard already. *Fuck. As if I didn't just get laid the other day...* He shifted to adjust himself in his pocket, then resumed watching Jackson work.

"Something like... this."

Chase swallowed and looked back at the hilt, which was condensed now. "Oh, wow," he whispered. Somehow, he'd tuned out the last minute of Jackson's work completely. He'd been too focused on watching his body move fluidly with his tools, like he'd been born with them in his hands.

He burned for the same kind of firm, certain touches.

Now, the strands of metal swooped around each other in a tighter space. They were hammered closer together as the whole half-sphere of metal seemed shorter but wider, offering more space underneath. It was cooling off, back to dark gray all over with only hints of red lines along the insides of the twists.

"It's only a rough prototype--"

"I love it," Chase whispered, his eyes lingering on all the details.

A smile broke across Jackson's face. "Yeah? We'll decide on the look of your blade and the grip next."

Jackson loosened the clamp and set the metal aside on the table, then slipped his gloves off.

Chase instinctively picked up the portfolio to offer Jackson. Instead, he found Jackson stepping closer – into his personal space bubble. Jackson waited for just a moment, his eyes flickering between Chase's with the question.

Chase stepped closer, too.

Jackson's hand cupped his chin, his thumb resting against the edge of Chase's jaw. He leaned down the two inches that separated them and their lips met.

Oh, yes.

He hadn't been kissed like this in... forever. Jackson's lips were warm and soft, the grip of his fingers rough and firm.

Chase pushed himself against Jackson's body and crushed himself close to kiss Jackson *hard*. His hand rose to run up

Jackson's back. Chase shivered at the muscles he felt along Jackson's back and shoulder blades. He boldly rested the other hand in the curve of Jackson's lower back, just above his ass.

Jackson's hand closed around the back of Chase's head. He caressed his neck and shoulder. Chase could feel him, half-hard, pressing into his thigh through layers of jeans.

Chase wanted that.

He sucked on Jackson's lower lip, his eyes flickering open. Jackson's delicate lashes fluttered up close with distant pleasure as his chest rose and fell quickly.

Every time Chase flicked his tongue across the skin or nipped it, Jackson's breathing caught in his chest. It was fucking sexy to watch.

Chase ran one hand up along Jackson's stomach and chest now, taking his time to feel the hard muscles under his palm. Fuck, he was built like a Greek god. He slipped his hand under Jackson's shirt and Jackson shivered at first, then pressed forward into Chase's hand.

When his fingertips brushed Jackson's nipple, Jackson's whole body clenched for a moment. Their thighs pressed together firmly enough that he felt Jackson's cock twitching. That was the *sexiest fucking thing.*

Chase wasn't ashamed to admit Jackson was getting to him more than any guy in recent history. He wanted to make Jackson feel good, take his mind off work and stress...

He gave Jackson a few last lingering kisses. Their teeth and tongues and lips worked together as they breathed hard. Chase's body burned with desire to be lifted off his feet and fucked by this man against the nearest wall. Instead, he shoved Jackson's chest until he'd backed him up against it. He dropped to his knees on the hard concrete floor.

"Oh, Christ," Jackson whispered. His barrel-like chest heaved with arousal as he reached down to rub himself through denim. "You're so fucking *hot*, Chase."

Chase grinned. "Sure that's not the forge?" It was hot in here, especially in the dead of August, but he didn't only want to strip down because of *that*. Watching Jackson's passion come out in every little movement had turned the simmering heat under his skin up to an uncontrollable boil.

"Funny." Jackson sucked in another quiet breath. Chase unbuttoned his jeans, slid the zipper down, and tugged them down a little before he pulled down the waistband. The base of his shaft came into view.

God, he was big.

The full length was well over his hand width, so he gripped the shaft and stroked it. The pink head gleamed. The rounded tip looked deliciously moist from grinding himself off against Chase's hip.

The distinctively salty taste of pre-come hit his tongue as he leaned in to run the flat of his tongue across the head.

Jackson kneaded his shoulders the whole time. Barely-restrained noises, probably stifled moans, slipped through the air.

That was all the encouragement he needed to dip his head and run his tongue tip from shaft to tip, around, and back down again.

The velvety weight in his hand stiffened at the extra attention, going from half-mast to fully erect in almost the blink of an eye. The stiffening under his mouth and the very close-up view were the hottest.

Jackson's thighs tensed and his stomach tightened. His fingertips dug into the flesh of Chase's shoulder. The second time Chase did that, another quiet grunt escaped the back of

Jackson's throat. He shifted his weight from foot to foot, biting back whatever words he had.

Chase scooted closer between Jackson's legs and knelt up a little straighter. Oh, the size of this delicious cock! When he licked back up to the head, this time, he closed his lips around the flushed head. He sucked at the sensitive slit for a moment, then kept his lips tight around the shaft. He bobbed his head down.

"Y-Yeah..." Jackson breathed out hoarsely. He kneaded Chase's shoulder rhythmically now. Fingernails dug into Chase's shoulder and he knew he was on the right track.

Chase took in the hot, throbbing shaft easily. He tilted his head just a little further with each inch to make sure it slid across his tongue to the back of his throat. He sucked in his cheeks, bobbing his head back up, then set into a quicker rhythm up and down the shaft.

Jackson's thighs quivered. He slid his hand up from Chases' shoulder to tangle in the hair at the back of Chase's head. He probably so desperately wanted to fuck Chase's mouth, but he stopped himself. His breathing came in short gasps as Chase sucked his cock.

Chase flickered his gaze up Jackson's body for the first time.

Sure, Jackson was stunning normally, but Jackson was indescribably beautiful leaning up against the wall, his legs spread. The back of one hand was on the wall above his head. His biceps were rippling, and his chest heaved. His gaze was focused on Chase.

"Mmm," Chase moaned around the shaft, flickering his tongue around the head. He teased that sensitive spot underneath the shaft before continuing to draw his mouth up and down.

Jackson growled under his breath. His cock was throbbing, so hot and salty, with just a hint of bitterness. His hips kept moving in the tiniest jerks like he was forcing them back against the wall despite himself. Chase let one hand rest on Jackson's hip and tugged it. He kept his head still and glanced up at him to encourage him to move.

"You sure?"

Chase's eyes narrowed with amusement, but he kept his mouth wrapped around the base of Jackson's cock. His nose was buried in the hair at the base of the shaft. *My mouth's a bit full, you.*

Jackson's cheeks were red as he pushed his hips forward once, then twice... A few thrusts later, he got into the rhythm of it.

Fuck, the only thing better would be having this hot man grab his cheeks harder. Chase wanted to feel his desperate desire to squirt his passion down Chase's throat...

As Jackson approached the edge, his balls drew tighter and his breathing stuttered more. His hips moved faster and it was harder to breathe.

Chase didn't give a fuck. Jackson was the hottest guy he'd sucked off in years, and he wasn't going to let bodily needs get in his way.

"You – you gotta finish," Jackson whispered moments later. His voice was hoarse and broken with pleasure. "Or else I'm gonna bruise your throat."

Chase nearly laughed, but he managed not to. He just pressed his palm to Jackson's stomach to slam him back against the wall. He aggressively sucked in his lips around the shaft again, bobbing his head up and down. He wanted to give him quick, ruthless enveloping warmth and wetness that he was certain would get Jackson there...

Jackson's groan echoed around the workshop. His hips pushed forward again and stuttered, thighs and stomach clenching. Chase's hand was still pressed against Jackson's chest, and he playfully tweaked Jackson's nipple.

"Y-Yes, oh, *fuck*, yes!" Jackson grunted. His shaft swelled, pulsated, and then... quick squirts of that glorious liquid, milky and thick and rich, almost sweet. It was the same baking soda base taste as every other guy, but there was something a little different, too.

Chase's fingertip trailed around Jackson's nipple and played over the nub lightly. "Hnh!" Jackson's whole body shivered with apparently pleasurable over stimulation.

Chase's throat bobbed. He swallowed each splatter of liquid against the back of his tongue and throat. He kept his mouth tight and bobbed his head to ease Jackson through his climax.

When Jackson's hips went still and his breathing started to steady, Chase finally drew his mouth off the softening shaft. Chase knelt back to wipe his mouth and swallow a few more times.

"Oh, Jesus, Chase," Jackson whispered, his eyes wide. His cheeks were still red, his stomach heaving as he tried to catch his breath.

Chase loved that reaction. It was like Jackson didn't take a second of what Chase had done for granted.

"Th-Thanks," Jackson added with a shaky laugh, and Chase laughed, too. How sweet.

He took Jackson's offered hand and rose to his feet. "No problem," he teased.

Already, reality set in again. He was so hard himself, but he could wait 'til he got home. He hadn't meant to be so pushy, to demand Jackson's kisses and his pleasure... Jackson was still staring at him wide-eyed as he tucked his cock back into his jeans.

I just fucked up our friendship, didn't I?

"Uh, I should probably get going..." Chase didn't even fully understand *why* he had the strong desire to flee; he just did.

"Wait," Jackson murmured as Chase took a step back. He stepped forward to stay close, reaching out to take Chase's hand. "May I please return the favor?"

What? Chase hadn't expected that.

"Uh..."

"I'd like to, if you're okay with it," Jackson added firmly. His gaze flickered between Chase's eyes. The way he watched Chase like he *knew* him, knew all the fears and worries playing on his mind... It was almost unnerving, but it was blindingly hot at the same time.

Chase swallowed hard. "Okay," he whispered, barely even sure what he was agreeing to. It had been ages since a guy had blown him, longer still since he'd come from it. Fuck, this could be so awkward.

Then again, he'd already taken the most awkward step in their relationship. He'd grabbed Jackson, kissed him, and sucked him off on the spot. Jackson couldn't possibly make things *more* awkward now.

And... something about Jackson made him feel secure enough to agree to it.

It's like I know him already. That sounds crazy. I can't tell him that.

"You're gorgeous," Jackson whispered. For a moment, Chase saw Antonio from the club the other night. But Jackson was watching him in the light of day – well, of the workshop – and asking him so politely if he could suck him off.

Chase knew he was blushing. He shifted from foot to foot, caught off guard and not sure what to say to that. "Th-Thanks," he laughed. "Glad I give such good head."

"Oh, you do," Jackson marveled. A smile curled his lips as he pressed close to Chase, his hands tracing down Chase's sides. Jackson's hands, when they squeezed his ass, were immensely distracting.

Chase shivered, pressing his thigh into Jackson's leg and grinding against him.

Then, Jackson's hands curled around his upper thighs, right by his ass, lifting him right off his feet.

"Oh, fuck," Chase exclaimed. He grabbed Jackson's shoulders as Jackson carried him across the workshop to the table where he'd been sitting with the portfolio.

Jackson laughed, shoving Chase onto his back on the table. He swept his portfolio book onto the chair. "You like your men big and strong, don't you?" he teased.

"Yeah." Chase's cheeks burned at the memory of Jackson looking at his sketches, looking back at his own and comparing them to Chase's body. Chase had done the same with his own sketches and Jackson's body...

Even knowing Jackson was into his type, he hadn't known Jackson was into *him*. And they might have only been casual friends, but this man was a catch.

"And good with their hands?" Jackson cupped his bulge through denim, his strong palm rubbing along the hardened shaft.

Chase rolled his head back with a moan of need. His toes curled into his shoes as he hooked his legs around the legs of the table.

Jackson crouched over him. He leaned across the table, bracing one strong arm over his head to kiss him hard.

In response, Chase grabbed Jackson's cheeks and pulled him closer. Their lips melded once more into a smooth, erotic dance of warm skin teasing skin. Jackson's kisses made his skin light up. Every nerve ending was suddenly more sensitive to Jackson's nipples brushing his own, or Jackson's hand wandering up his stomach...

"Oh, my – oh my God," Chase moaned, his cock aching. His head spun at what it was like to be touched and cherished, and not just in the moments before getting fucked. If Jackson could do *that* again already, he'd was a miracle or he was lying about his age.

But Jackson wasn't out for pleasure for himself. The thought was nearly overwhelming. Chase let go of Jackson, thrilled that Jackson kept kissing him in rough, wet, open-mouthed kisses. He ran his hands up over Jackson's rippling arms and down his back. Jackson's body was warm and pleasurable against his needy erection, but it wasn't enough.

"Oh, God, please," Chase moaned. Jackson slid a little further away, kissing his way – tortuously slow – down Chase's body. Chase squirmed against the table. He wished those lips were wrapping around his bare nipple or pressed against bare skin... Jackson teased him through his shirt, all the way down to his stomach.

Jackson crouched over his groin. He raised his hips to let Jackson unbutton his jeans and slide them down to his thighs. His cock popped free in the warm air, his heart pounding with nervous anticipation.

Roughened fingers slid up under his shirt this time, feeling him up just as he'd touched Jackson in the heat of the moment. Unlike Chase had done, Jackson didn't tease him, though.

A hot, almost unbearably stimulating mouth closed around the tip of his cock. Then, Chase was enveloped by that same wet heat all the way down his shaft. His whole body throbbed and thrummed with desire. "Y-Yes...!"

Jackson groaned quietly. The vibrations sent little shivers through Chase's thighs as he braced his feet around the edge of the table legs. It kept him almost flat on the table... Almost. Not so he couldn't push up once or twice between those supple, smooth lips, though.

It was impossible to hold out for long under this attention. The wet heat sucking tightly around his sensitive skin was hard to handle. Then, Jackson pulled his head back to rub the rest of the shaft with one hand and firmly suck the tip...

Yet Chase couldn't quite finish, still so wrapped up in his own anxiety and inexperience. His heart pounded and his chest heaved for breath. It was like he was hanging on the precipice. His whole body quivered or flinched every time Jackson's touch ignited nerves along his skin or made his stomach tense. But he couldn't quite get there.

His chest pounded harder and harder with nameless worries, even as his body still quivered on that knife's edge of need. A couple of minutes of torture later, he whispered, "Christ, I might – I might take a while..."

Jackson sucked his mouth off the length and licked it as he whispered, "That's all right." His voice rumbled in a deep, desiring growl. "I got all night."

Oh, fuck, of course he was patient and sweet and so fucking hot...

And he sounded like he'd meant it. Chase relaxed against

the table again, sharply moaning when Jackson's wet mouth enveloped him again.

This time, within minutes, he felt tingles building under his skin. The electric chills were so welcome. He relished them, grinning as he rolled his head back and squeezed his eyes shut. As his cock twitched, his muscles quivering, he clenched his hand around Jackson's shoulder. "Nnh...! Oh, J-Jackson...! Yes!"

Jackson's warm wetness was enough to take him over the edge. Jackson kept bobbing his head as Chase unconsciously thrust his hips. Chase opened his eyes enough to hazily watch... and Jackson was watching *him* like the most beautiful thing he'd ever had on his workshop table.

Chase's cheeks were already flushed, his chest rising and falling rapidly. "Oh, man," he whispered as Jackson pulled his head up and swallowed again. It was a good thing he was sprawled across the table. He felt utterly boneless for the few moments it took to pull himself together.

Then, he grunted and hauled himself up again. He sat up straight, unhooking his feet from around the table legs to pull his jeans up again. "Okay, I better head out now. See you soon, yeah?"

Jackson stood back to allow him space to pass, smiling. He seemed sincere as he nodded. "See you soon."

Chase's hands shook as he pulled the workshop door shut behind himself. He walked down the dirt driveway to the sidewalk and shoved them into his pockets.

What have I done?

That familiar pit of self-loathing was gone. This time... he felt good, and he wasn't sure how to handle it.

CHAPTER
Fourteen

JACKSON

By Friday, two days later, Jackson was still thinking about Chase. That gorgeous, intense, sweet man who'd writhed in pleasure on his workshop table wouldn't get out of his mind.

He'd told himself he was looking for a boyfriend, not a hookup, but that...

That had been *good*.

He didn't try to fool himself into thinking it would be that good with some other random guy, though. It never had been before.

No. This was about Chase. Somehow, Jackson was already crushing on Chase a lot harder than he'd thought... and it was mutual! Why hadn't he picked up on it before?

He'd been excited when the cool, out-of-town artist had agreed to meet up with him for the first time for coffee. And when they'd agreed to make it a regular thing. And each time he'd spotted Chase waiting for him at the coffee shop table.

After flirting at the art show, Jackson had just backed off

because... well... he didn't have a good reason, really. He'd just focused on work instead, and renovations, and everything but dating.

Had Chase been harboring the same quiet flame all along? Maybe that was projecting his own feelings. Chase might not even want more than a one-time hookup.

That actually worried Jackson. Chase was acting weird. He hadn't texted Jackson in the last few days, and he'd definitely run away after their hookup. Jackson had let him go. Chase's emotions might play havoc with him if he had some kind of awful ex stuff going on, after all. Now he wondered if he should have asked Chase to stay and talk it out.

But man, if he could hand over the perfect finished sword and win Chase's heart... He allowed himself a romantic daydream or two as he threw everything into finishing those railings for Cam's house.

That weekend, Cameron was out at Noah's being lovey-dovey, which was perfect timing. With Thomas's help, he used his spare key to get into Cameron's house and haul the last few pieces inside. They were spending Saturday afternoon installing them.

Thomas seemed to enjoy sawing through the old posts. They worked a section at a time to pull out the crappy old wooden railings and balusters. Then, they hauled up a section of the new wrought iron ones to install.

It was hard work. By the time they'd worked their way down to the last section along the stairs, Thomas was worn out. "I'm gonna grab a breather."

"Getting hot in here, isn't it? We need AC," Jackson laughed. "You go get fresh air."

Once Thomas was out, he went about testing the railings

and measuring. He made sure everything was flawlessly installed while his mind wandered again to Chase.

Thomas came back in a minute later. "Someone here to see you," he told Jackson, his lips tugging up in a little smile.

"Oh?" Jackson wasn't expecting anyone. He knew who he *hoped* it was, but it probably wasn't. "We're done here once we clean up all the shavings and polish the railings..."

"We can do that tomorrow," Thomas laughed. "I'm done and you should be, too."

Jackson grinned and rose to his feet to head for the front door. "Yes, boss. Lock up?"

"Yep."

When Jackson headed down Cameron's driveway, he saw what Thomas meant.

Chase was hanging around his front door, kicking the step as he turned this way and that. Even from a distance, he looked nervous... but cute.

Always cute.

"Hey," Jackson greeted with a broad smile. "How are you doing?"

"Um, good," Chase answered. He didn't smile back yet, and stress lines had formed around his eyes. His hands were tucked into his pockets, his body swaying a little from side to side. "Can we talk for a bit?"

He was breathing heavily, his lips swollen and his eyes dark and fixed right on Jackson.

Does he want to hook up again? A moment of annoyance flashed through Jackson: it would be hard to say no, but he wouldn't agree to a string of booty calls. Even if it was Chase. Probably.

"Sure," he answered. He passed Chase to open his front door and let him in.

Chase followed him to the living room and dropped onto the couch next to him. Jackson had half-expected him to sit on his lap. "I'm sorry I ran out on you."

"Oh, no. It's all right," Jackson told him, but his curiosity was ignited. Chase was admitting to doing that? What was going on? "Can I ask... what that was about, though?"

"I was nervous," Chase admitted. He'd drawn his hands out of his pockets and he was fidgeting with his fingers in his lap. "*Am* nervous," he corrected himself.

Jackson raised his eyebrows, remaining calm so he didn't startle Chase. "Oh, yeah? Well, you don't have to be. We can play it cool if you want."

"That was the first time in ages a guy reciprocated. And I just... uh... Do you want a date?"

Jackson wasn't expecting that. *Is he interested, or is he just offering to be polite?* "If that's what you want, too, yeah. You don't owe me one." The look Chase gave him, his brows slightly furrowed and those cute lips parted slightly, made Jackson think nobody had said that.

"No," Chase agreed a few moments later. "I suppose I don't, but I... I like you."

Jackson's heart soared. He tried to hide his feelings, but he knew he was an open book. Everyone teased him for it. He was already smiling as he watched Chase. Following his instincts, Jackson leaned in. "Can I kiss you?"

"Oh, yeah." Chase shook out the nervous jitters with a quick laugh and leaned in to press his lips against Jackson's.

The kiss was short and sweet this time. Jackson took his time gently sliding and caressing his lips against Chase's. When they pulled back, their eyes fluttered open again as they stayed close to one another. Chase's arm brushed against Jackson's shoulder. The sparks that ignited made Jackson want to hug him and slide closer.

Chase looked much calmer now, his shoulders down and his muscles loose again. "Cool."

"Very cool," Jackson agreed with a grin. "You're really cute. I didn't think you were into me..."

"I didn't think *you* were into *me!*" Chase rebutted, and Jackson laughed. "When did that happen?"

Jackson shrugged. "I thought you were cool from when we first met at the show."

"Three months later... you slow-played that one," Chase laughed. He pulled himself up to his feet. "I don't want to run, but I gotta get to work and then fencing... I just wanted to stop by and sort us out first."

Jackson stood up again, too, to walk Chase to the door. "I'm glad you did. What's your work schedule like?"

"All over the place, and fencing classes too... but I'm off on Monday night."

Jackson could be free any night he wanted, so he nodded. "That conveyor belt sushi place has Monday night specials..."

"Yes, please!" Chase exclaimed. "I've been dying to go out for sushi with someone. Floyd hates fish."

Jackson burst out laughing. "Oh. Well, I'm glad I can fill a sushi niche."

"You can fill..." Chase actually stopped and blushed, which made Jackson stare. He wouldn't have held back the comment before. Something was different. "Never mind."

Jackson swatted Chase's arm playfully. "Naughty. Get out of here. Don't be late for work."

Chase laughed again and leaned in and up to peck his lips. He nearly pulled the door open in his own face in his rush to get out the door. Jackson bit back a laugh, leaning in the doorway to watch him jog down the street, smiling all the way.

That broody, anxious air was gone, and Jackson was glad to see it go.

Fifteen

CHASE

"Oh, my God," Chase mumbled to himself for about the dozenth time that day. All through his work shift, he'd been consumed by thoughts of the upcoming date on Monday. Floyd had eyed him when he came in to take the evening shift but he let Chase go without asking him why he was beaming.

Chase couldn't believe he'd pushed through his anxiety. He'd actually come back to Jackson and asked for a date.

Still, his anxiety was there. *I haven't been on a date in ages. What the hell am I doing?*

When he silenced that part of himself, the answer was clear: he was following his instincts. Jackson was worth a date. If only just to see how it went.

Once Chase got back to his apartment building, he let himself into the lobby. He fumbled around to find his key and check the mailbox. Probably just bills and junk, but he had to pay them sometime.

He closed his fingers around a small stack of envelopes and glossy fliers and pulled them out. He rifled through them before he even shut his mailbox again. Fucking post office guy kept bringing grocery flyers he didn't want.

Chase went stock-still when he flipped past the flyer to a plain white envelope. There was familiar handwriting: *C. MacLeod.*

"Oh, shit, no."

They found me.

His hand shook as he closed and locked his mailbox. He yanked the lobby door open and jogged up the stairs to his apartment just one floor up.

When did I last check it? Wednesday? Thursday?

Is this a warning?

Fuck, I should have been checking my mail daily, just in case. This was bound to happen...

Chase headed straight for his dining room table, tossed the rest of his mail aside, and opened the letter.

It was a single sheet, not even a full page, handwritten, and a newspaper clipping was enclosed.

Dear Charlie:

We've been thinking of you much lately and missing you. In a few months it will be the holidays. We hoped you'd have come around, but instead you have moved further away?? What is in New Brunswick for you? Your family is all here.

The congregation would welcome you back too. Fr. Williams has kindly agreed to help you find a better path. As you know, we are worried for your spiritual salvation. We have nothing against gay people; we just don't want our son to be one. We hate the sin but love the sinner. Your uncle has told you before how we feel but it bears repeating. Many people are doing good work in this field, see enclosed. You have the fortitude to become one of the lucky few to escape that path.

Luke misses you too. His grades include As in Math, Art, and

Bible Studies. You know he would love to hear from you again. He drew you a Thanksgiving card at Sunday school and we were going to enclose it but he wants to give it to you in person. Buddy is getting older but still plays with tennis balls like always. Sometimes he lies on your bed and won't come eat until we pray with him. Your aunt and uncle moved to Colorado, and Grandma asked about you the other day. Your uncle said he wishes he could get through to you again. He misses his nephew. Sad that we didn't have news to share.

Please stop running and come to God. We're waiting to welcome you with open arms.

Your loving family,

Mom, Dad, Luke, & Buddy

Chase wiped his eyes, throwing the letter on the table and drawing a deep breath as tears stung. This was the very fucking stereotype of what happened when a kid came out. Hilariously, hellishly, he was living it. Some people thought it was over these days, but obviously not.

He wished he could say he hated his parents for writing the letter, or for using his little brother and dog against him. For tracking him down when he'd moved to *another fucking province* and changed his name and left *everything* to escape their phone calls, visits, emails, prayers...

But he didn't.

He just hated what they'd become.

Chase swallowed back his bitter words, stomping over to the coffee table to grab a pen. He leaned over the dining room table and, in huge letters, scrawled over the letter.

I am a fag.

His lip curled, he repeated the phrase over and over in smaller text. He wrote sideways across the letter to blot out everything they'd written.

I am a fag. I am a fag. I am a fag...

By the time he got to the bottom edge of the paper, his hand was cramping from holding the pen so tightly. The angry tears stinging at his eyes had given way to pure fury ripping through his bones.

How *dare* they try to guilt him? How dare they use his little brother, ten years old and already being indoctrinated by those bastards, against him? How dare they throw those words at him and now pretend to care about him?

First, they could answer for what they'd done. Then, *maybe* in another few years, he'd consider talking to them.

Chase's hands shook as he shoved the paper back into the envelope along with the clipping about some reparative therapy bullshit. He taped it shut, crossed out the address, and wrote his old home address on it. He had to search his junk drawer for a good minute before he found stamps. He slapped one on and strode down to the post box at the end of the street to drop it in. When the handle slammed shut, his letter swallowed by the system, he didn't regret it for a second.

For the first time since he'd read the letter, he took a long, deep breath. He let it out, pushing away from the post box again.

It was a warm summer evening. Maybe he'd eat out on his balcony.

As he pushed his empty bowl back across the flimsy plastic table, Chase licked the last few Sidekicks away from the insides of his cheeks. They were great for creamy, flat noodles, but they left an annoying feeling in his mouth.

He leaned back in his lawn chair, looking out over the lights of the apartment building across from them. He could see a small park and the parking lot. It wasn't the best view. Most people here didn't use their balconies except to store bikes.

Chase didn't care how bad the view was; he'd never had a balcony in an apartment before. Being able to step outside into fresh air, especially over the warm summer, was nice. Nothing like what Jackson and his brothers had going on, though... He was a little jealous.

He raised his thumb to his mouth to nibble at his nail absently, then jerked his hand away. He didn't want to get into that habit again. But of all the coping habits, at least nail biting wouldn't kill him.

Instead, he grabbed his phone and opened his string of texts with Jackson. The glow almost blinded him now that his eyes had adjusted to the darkness. He carefully typed out a new one.

Still on for Monday?

It was a hint as much as a question. Chase couldn't stand the thought of dragging Jackson into his shit. The thought of what could happen... And he didn't want anyone else looking at him with pity. Pity was one step away from disgust. Worse yet, one step away from 'what's wrong with you that they threw you out?' and the thoughts that crept into his mind after midnight.

It wasn't that late yet, and the answer was almost immediate.

I'm on. Monday at 6pm? :)

Chase worked his jaw around. His stomach churned with anxiety as he brought his bowl and fork back inside and locked his balcony door. Then, he sent a simple response.

Sure :)

At least Jackson seemed like a decent guy, and honest. He wasn't out to use Chase. Maybe Chase could find some way to make a relationship work. They could even just be friends-with-benefits, if Jackson wanted something stable.

Chase could do just sex. He knew he was good at *that*, and he would happily fall into bed with Jackson every fuckin' day of the week.

But sex aside, what did Jackson think Chase could give him? And was he right? Last week, Chase would have said he didn't want – couldn't do – romance. Now... he wasn't so sure.

CHAPTER
Sixteen

THOMAS

THOMAS PAUSED AND SQUINTED DOWN THE ROAD, HIS HAND ON the little red flag on his mailbox.

That was a police car pulling away from the curb, and a flicker of movement on Cameron's porch caught his eye. Cam and Noah were standing outside, talking between themselves.

Thomas flicked down the red flag. He bundled the newspaper under his arm and crossed through the bushes to his brother's driveway. "Hey – what happened? Was that here?"

"Yeah," Cameron frowned. "At Jackson's. Someone complained about the smoke from his forge."

Thomas's eyes narrowed. "No. *Wood* smoke?"

"Apparently. The cop didn't take it too seriously," Noah murmured. Thomas liked him – he was grounded, sweet, and smart. A touch feminine, but they shared a certain appreciation for life outside the strict little box of masculinity. They had always got along well.

For once, Noah was in old, faded jeans and a t-shirt. That was rare.

"But who reported him?"

"A neighbor, apparently. I got to the cop before he got to Jackson, but Jackson's gonna be *pissed*."

Thomas's eyes were drawn back to his own house, then the house on the other side. "I bet I know who it was."

Cathy and Don, the couple on the other side, were stand-offish. Several other neighbors had come to greet them, all amused or admiring their living situation, but they hadn't. They hadn't even waved when Thomas saw them on Friday morning before work. How rude.

"You think?"

"It's my best guess. Everyone else has been great. Occam's Razor."

Noah chuckled, but Cam rolled his eyes. "Don't talk smart people to me. All right, d'you think we should talk to them?"

"It might look a bit intimidating," Thomas frowned.

Noah stifled his laugh and Thomas glanced at him. "Sorry. Just... the two of us a little less than him..."

Cameron folded his arms, his biceps flexing. He hadn't been able to train since he'd been diagnosed with CPVT. The doctors had promptly changed their order of "don't exercise hard" to "don't exercise at all until after surgery." Even so, Cam still had more muscles than Thomas. Just like Jackson, his two brothers were built big and strong, and he'd been the runt since birth.

Thomas laughed. "Yeah, true."

"How about a barbecue?" Noah suggested.

"A... what? We've been having them all summer," Cam frowned.

Noah gestured around. "No, a community one. Hold one for the neighborhood. Once we finish pulling down all the fence, we'll have enough room. Make it an end-of-summer event, you know?"

"I like that idea." Thomas could already see the potential – bribing their neighbors with food and handmade items. They could get to know Cathy and Don a little. Assuming they weren't homophobic assholes, they could cut off the problem at its root.

Nobody else had had a problem with the wood stove all summer. In a few months' time, everyone would be burning wood, too, as the days grew chillier. They just needed to make peace for now.

A smirk spread over Cam's face. "On that note, I could use a hand..."

Thomas eyed him. "With what?"

"Oh, god, you had to ask," Noah laughed. "Go get work jeans on."

Thomas blew out a sigh. He trotted down the steps and over to his house. As much as he didn't enjoy physical labor, he, Jackson, and Noah had all picked up some slack for Cam. Cam's heart condition was worse than the doctors had first suspected. None of them were letting him overwork himself, as frustrated as he was about it.

He joined the other two in the backyard a few minutes later, this time in old jeans and a t-shirt like Noah.

Cameron was hovering around near Noah, his hands rising. He looked like he wanted to help Noah lever the crowbar between the board and the fence.

"Go sit down," Thomas ordered.

"Fine," Cameron laughed. He sank into the lawn chair nearby and crossed his ankle over his knee, but still knelt forward to watch Noah work.

It was killing Cam not to be active. A shiver ran down

Thomas's spine at the thought and he sharply reprimanded himself. That was hyperbole, but it might actually kill Cam *to* be active.

"What's going on? Work party? This early on a Sunday?" Jackson was already in work clothes as he stepped through the fence separating Thomas's house from his own. He walked through Thomas's yard toward the fence between Cam's and Thomas's places.

"Yep, come join us," Thomas told him. "They put me to work, you can put those burly arms to use for once."

Jackson laughed and smacked his shoulder. He took the pry bar out of his hand. "Let me do that part, string bean. And *I* did most of the sneaky railing installation."

"I still can't believe you guys blindsided me with that," Cameron marveled. "I walked in and nearly passed out." At least he was joking about his condition now.

They all laughed, and Jackson pointed Thomas a few feet away. "You hammer out the nails. We're saving that wood."

Thomas glanced over at Cameron and raised his eyebrows. *Should we tell him?*

Cam shook his head.

Jackson didn't even notice the exchange. He was buoyant, humming cheerily as he started prying boards out of the fence. One at a time, he handed them over to have the nails hammered out and be stacked up neatly. He ripped boards out easily when he had to. Thomas was privately glad he was taking over that bit.

"Someone had a good night," Thomas observed with a smirk. He'd last seen Jackson going into his house with Chase, but Chase had left not long afterward. Was that what this was about? The way Jackson's eyes flickered to Cam and Noah before him told him he was exactly right.

"What, a man's not allowed to have good cheer in his own yard? Especially at a work party?" Jackson handed over a board and winked.

Thomas couldn't help a laugh. "Fine, be optimistic before noon. But don't expect me to be."

"It's eleven-thirty. You're running out of time," Noah observed.

Thomas groaned. "Smart-ass."

Noah smirked at Cameron, sharing some inside joke at that response.

They worked well together to pry out the rest of the boards along that side of the fence. They only snapped a few and saved a good chunk of them. When Jackson started carrying the lumber to his yard to store, Thomas pitched in. He wanted to help out just to get a chance to talk to him.

"You talked to Chase, huh?"

Jackson gave a rueful grin. "That obvious?"

Thomas coughed. "Uh, you're kind of beaming like the sun..."

"I'm never subtle," Jackson lamented. "I got a date with Chase."

Thomas's eyebrows shot up. He *hadn't* been imagining the chemistry between them at the barbecue! He pumped his fist. "I knew it."

Jackson punched his shoulder lightly. "Fuck off. A gay guy can have male friends, you know..."

"Yeah, you have plenty. You don't sidle your way up to them like a teenage girl fluttering her eyelashes..." Thomas widened his eyes like Jackson's had been whenever he listened to Chase talk.

Jackson was bright red now, but he laughed. "You asshole. I thought you'd mock me less than Cam and Noah..."

"I'll be good," Thomas promised, laughing. He raised his hands once he set down the load of lumber. "I promise. Keep me updated."

"I will." Despite his embarrassment, Jackson still glowed. He walked in a pleased, rolling stride, still humming under his breath.

It was good to see him like this. Thomas couldn't remember when Jackson had last been in love or even crushing hard. It was just like Cam had been around Noah in the spring. That left him as the only single brother.

Not everything between us has to be a competition. Thomas shook his head and followed Jackson back to his yard.

CHAPTER
Seventeen

JACKSON

O̶N̶ MONDAY NIGHT, JACKSON SHUT DOWN HIS FORGE AN HOUR early just to head inside, shower, and shave. Maybe half his appeal was working hard in the workshop, but this was a first date. He wanted to be clean and presentable.

Jackson shrugged on his usual gray t-shirt, then browsed his closet. He didn't want to choose plaid – too casual. A white shirt was too formal. Something in between...

After a few moments of thought, he picked out a long-sleeved dark purple collared shirt. He added a gray zip-up sweater in case the evening was chilly.

"That's it."

Paired with black jeans, Jackson was good to go.

He strode out and locked the door to walk to the sushi restaurant. He could have driven, but it really wasn't far away and he was starting to like walking back and forth more to town. This neighborhood was only a couple minutes closer than his old house but it felt like a much bigger difference.

By the time he reached the sushi restaurant, it was six on the nose. Chase stood outside, browsing his phone.

"Hey! Did I keep you? Sorry!"

Chase automatically smiled, pocketing his phone and reaching out to touch Jackson's arm. "Hi. No, not at all. I just got here." He leaned into Jackson and tilted his chin up, so Jackson leaned down to peck him on the lips. *He's so bold. I love it.*

"All right. Shall we head in?"

They took seats at a table next to the conveyor belt. Jackson rolled his shoulders and scooted in next to it to get a good look at what was going around. "How was your weekend?"

"Slow," Chase admitted. "Work went pretty well, though."

Jackson nodded. "Mine was pretty slow, too. I spent yesterday pulling out the fence between my brothers' houses. The one between Thomas and me is the next to go."

Chase raised his eyebrow. "Just... ripping out fences bare-handed? Okay, Popeye."

Jackson was startled into a laugh. "I'm not casually boasting--"

The waiter interrupted them to deliver water and ask if they had any special orders. Jackson turned them down. It was more fun to hunt from the belt anyway.

"I wish they'd had cool stuff like this in university," Jackson lamented. "My buddies and I would have gone out all the time."

"You did uni here?"

"I did an associate's degree, yeah," Jackson told him. "Then I realized I was enjoying blacksmithing too much and I actually liked it. Why bother pursuing a useless degree and getting in debt for something I'll never use?"

Before he even finished the sentence, Chase was nodding hard. "Exactly. I did my freshman year at U of T in fine arts, and... Jesus, I blew so much money. Then I did a tattoo school and I got lucky enough to get an apprenticeship, and that actually gave me a career."

"D'you ever feel you missed out?" Jackson asked.

Chase frowned. "A little, sometimes. I mean, some guys wound up becoming socially aware, getting involved in activism and nonprofits and stuff. But a lot of others just... integrated into whatever other jobs we could find. I wish I'd been able to study queer studies as a major. I might've liked that."

"Yeah," Jackson hummed. He took his time to work through the three plates he'd first grabbed. "I don't know, I'm glad I went, but I'm also glad I didn't finish."

"What was the associate's degree in?"

"Metal processing."

Chase looked blank. He finished his last roll and started watching the belt again. "Like... what?"

"Uh, basically, I could be a welder or a ship-builder or something."

"Oh. So that tied in with your blacksmith stuff. That's a lot more useful than an arts degree..." Chase grabbed another plate from the belt. "Aha. I knew there was another one of these going around.

Jackson laughed, then shrugged. "Even your year taught you some stuff for tattooing, though, I bet?"

"Yeah," Chase admitted. He smiled, setting down his chopsticks to drink a few sips of water. "I like that you take my art seriously."

Jackson stacked up his empty plates and folded his arms, leaning back to watch Chase. "Of course I do. I'm in the same boat. Most people think I just make swords..." Chase blushed. "Not you," he hurried to reassure Chase. "But most people."

Chase nodded. "Before I talked to you, I kinda thought so, too. I had this image of, I don't know, a manly burly dude with a foot-long beard and a Viking longship in his backyard..."

Jackson started to laugh. He might have been pretty strong, but he wasn't into the reenactment scene like his weaponry customers. "Yeah, no, that's common."

"Kinda like most people think tattoo artists are ultra-masculine bikers. I'm girly in that scene," Chase sighed.

Jackson frowned sympathetically. "Yeah. A little like Noah, then...?"

Chase winced. "I guess."

There it is. Jackson leaned forward. "Sorry. Is there something bad between you two...?"

"No, no," Chase hastened to answer, almost spilling his water glass. "Crap. Oh, I didn't spill it." He pushed aside his empty plates, then stacked them up to make room, his eyes down on the plates.

Jackson gave him a few moments to decide how to answer since something was clearly bothering him. He'd noticed something weird between them at the barbecue.

"I just... I have trouble with really... fem guys," Chase admitted. "Christ, that sounds bad, but it's just..."

"Internalized shit? We've all been there."

Chase winced again and nodded. "Yeah, I guess. I *like* Noah, it's just... you know, he'd never fly in my hometown."

I thought he was from Toronto.

Jackson sipped from his water glass. When Noah didn't seem inspired to continue, he answered, "Fair enough. As long as you treat him fine and vice versa, we're cool. It takes time to work out all that BS from your system."

"Oh, yeah. Of course! I'd never take out my own... issues...

on him," Chase promised. He met Jackson's eyes now with a frown of concern. "Sorry I'm being weird. It was just a rough weekend."

I'm not guilting him, am I? Jackson reached across the table to touch Chase's hand. "I know you wouldn't." Chase hesitantly smiled, and Jackson met it with a smile of his own. "Sorry you had a bad weekend, man."

"S'okay," Chase assured him. "It's a lot better Monday night, though." Chase didn't pull back from the touch, his gaze flickering between Jackson's eyes. He turned his palm over to rub his hand along Jackson's as they shared a few moments of silence. "Shall we continue eating? Or are you full off three rolls?"

"Hell, no, I'm not done," Jackson laughed. They turned their attention to grabbing plates from the belt again. Jackson started smiling again when he realized his hand still tingled from the brushes against Chase's palm.

The rest of their supper was far more relaxed. By the time he walked Chase home, they were bumping each other's sides playfully. Chase even reached out to take his hand for a few minutes while they walked and bantered.

Chase's weird moment earlier was truly gone, his wicked sense of humor back. Sometimes Jackson was left speechless, but he always ended up laughing. It was self-deprecating sometimes; Chase didn't take himself too seriously, and Jackson liked a grounded guy.

"You could come in," Chase offered, gesturing toward his apartment building. "I'd like that."

Jackson's eyes flickered between Chase's. Even the

prospect of pulling away from him and walking home right now felt... cold.

Even in the short second or two he thought about it, the burn under his skin told him he wanted Chase.

"Okay."

They were quiet now, the banter of moments ago gone as Chase led him to the staircase and up the flight of stairs. Every time they brushed, Jackson heard Chase's breath catch. He was sensitive even to Jackson reaching out to run a hand slowly up from the small of his back to the back of his neck.

He could be really fun in bed.

Jackson played with the hair at the back of Chase's head while Chase unlocked the door.

They took seconds to take their shoes off, their eyes fixed on each other.

"Want some water or something?" Chase asked to break the tension, his breathing already quick and his pupils blown wide. His eyes kept flickering up and down Jackson's body.

Jackson shook his head. He'd had his fill at the restaurant. He wanted a drink of *this* man, though.

"C'mon, then." Chase took his hand to lead him to the living room and plopped on the couch, then pulled Jackson down beside him. He casually yanked his shirt out by the front so it was untucked and unbuttoned the top button or two.

Jackson shifted to sit sideways, his arm along the back of the couch behind Chase. "You're really trying to tempt me, aren't you?" he teased.

Chase gave him a sly wink. "I might be. I've been waiting for hours now, you wanna kiss me again or what?"

Cocky! The demand made Jackson laugh out loud, a grin spreading over his face. "I suppose. If you insist."

He leaned in to press his lips against Chase's warm, pliable lips. Chase turned to press their knees together, already sliding his arm around Jackson's shoulders.

Jackson slid his arm around Chase's back in response, running his hand up Chase's back to the back of his neck again. He kissed Chase's lips a few times for thoroughness. Next, he started to kiss along his jaw to his ear.

A shiver wracked Chase, and Jackson grinned. "You're so much fun," he murmured into Chase's ear. He gently pressed a few kisses below and behind Chase's ear.

"O-Oh Jesus," Chase whispered, his nails digging into Jackson's shoulders.

He was so fucking sensitive, and Jackson loved it. He kept kissing along the rim of Chase's ear to his lobe. He flicked his tongue along it and Chase's body nearly melted in his arms. At the warm kiss to his pulse point on his neck, Chase shifted, his breath catching.

It only took a kiss or two at his collarbone before Chase fumbled to unbutton the rest of his shirt, shoving it wide open.

Jackson took a moment to admire his chest, nearly bare of tattoos around his pecs. It showed off a gorgeous piece: an old-fashioned clock with Roman numerals and some fluid lines around it. "Beautiful tattoo."

"Th-Thanks," Chase breathed out. His voice was hoarse already, his body arching toward Jackson. Jackson gently trailed his lips along the warm skin of Chase's collarbone.

Chase was already panting, tiny sounds escaping from the back of his throat. His body pulsed and shivered with pleasure as Jackson gently savored the warm, soft skin under his lips. Jackson's lips closed around his nipple just below the tattoo, and Chase gritted his teeth and just moaned.

Jackson flicked his tongue along the nub, then circled his tongue around it a few times before flicking it a bit harder.

"Jesus, Jackson," Chase whimpered, his nails biting *hard* into Jackson's shoulder now. It was a good thing Jackson had his shirt on.

He was *so* a scratcher... and maybe a screamer.

Jackson itched to find out.

He just chuckled and kissed over to the other one. He took his time to lick the bare skin around it before he licked the nipple and flicked it against his teeth.

Chase was sliding closer to him, pulling himself across the couch in an attempt to straddle Jackson's lap.

Jackson pulled back, his breathing heavy. "I don't want to leave you hanging. We should leave off before I get too far."

Chase groaned quietly. He touched his face to compose himself. "Yeah," he agreed breathily. "You're fuckin' addictive."

He was utterly, breathtakingly gorgeous, and Jackson was *hooked.*

"So are you. When you're not running," Jackson winked.

"I won't run next time," Chase mumbled, but he was blushing hard as he lowered his hands again. He turned his head so Jackson kissed his lips instead of his cheeks. "You're incredible."

Jackson chuckled, tangling a hand in Chase's hair and cupping his cheek.

God, it fit perfectly in his palm. He gently rubbed his fingertips through the hair above Chase's ear. He rubbed his thumb along Chase's jaw, watching his expressions with such affection. He pecked Chase's lips again and sat up to let him compose himself.

Chase murmured, "It's my turn, though. I owe you one..."

Jackson frowned. *Nope.* "No such thing as owing me," he told him firmly. "I don't want you counting favors."

Chase blushed again, his cheeks rounding in pleasure before he smiled. "C-Cool. You don't want to...?"

Jackson shook his head. "Not tonight," he murmured. "Another date? If you're up for it. You don't have to go on a date every time we make out. I mean, we're not exclusive. It can be a forging date."

Startled, Chase laughed. "No, I got that," he assured Jackson. "And no, we're not. But I... I think I'm cool with a forging date. That sounds hot. Haha."

Jackson snorted with laughter at the little pun. He reached out to cup Chase's cheek again, then rose to his feet. "All right. Tomorrow? Is that too soon?"

Chase laughed again. "Tomorrow's great," he murmured. The way his cheeks shone made Jackson suddenly realize what Thomas meant about him glowing.

Ohhh. The feeling's mutual.

Maybe Chase couldn't say it yet, but Jackson wasn't the only one wanting touch and affection just as much as sex – maybe more. Chase stood up to walk him to the door, and he took his hand. He rubbed his thumb down Jackson's, fidgeting with his fingers.

Chase didn't even seem to want to let go of his hand when they reached the door.

Jackson laughed gently. "You had a good time tonight?"

"Really good," Chase told him with another of those wholehearted smiles, finally letting go of his hand so he could pull on his shoes. "You?"

"I did." Jackson bent over to shove his shoes on again, then straightened up.

Chase looked adorable standing there all mussed up. His

hair was a mess, his eyes hazy and cheeks still pink with pleasure, a smile on his lips...

He was so irresistible.

Jackson slid his hands around Chase's hips and pulled him in to kiss him once more. "Okay. I don't really wanna go, but I should..." he laughed.

Chase was still grinning. "Me neither." He hesitated and added, "Been a while since I had a date this good."

"Me too."

Jackson brushed a hand over his face and shook his head. *Okay, snap out of it. God. It's like you're sixteen again.* He cleared his throat and pulled back from Chase, raising a hand to wave. "Tomorrow, yeah?"

"Definitely tomorrow," Chase confirmed, reaching out to hold the door for him.

Jackson waved once more before pulling open the staircase door to head back to his own house. For the first time in a while, he could see himself not just having sex after a date, but spending the evening afterward with this guy. He could see himself just holding him, playing with his hair, teasing him...

He was lost in Chase.

Eighteen

CHASE

THE FIRST HOUR AFTER JACKSON LEFT WAS THE BEST. CHASE tidied up his apartment and grinned at thoughts of their upcoming date tomorrow. He'd skip a fencing session for Jackson. After that point, as darkness fell over the city and the quiet of his apartment sank in, his mood started to sink.

It wasn't the same strange, stomach-grinding numbness as before. It was the growing feeling that something wasn't quite right. The more Chase tried to ignore it, the worse it got.

"Christ," he finally muttered as he grabbed a beer bottle and turned on the TV to try to find a distraction.

It wasn't fair. Jackson always worked to pleasure him and make him feel utterly comfortable and secure. They hadn't even hooked up, for Christ's sake, and he was still left feeling like this.

What was up with that?

A beer later, he thought he had it untangled: *something* fucked him up about feeling desirable. He'd thought that was one of the things he most wanted. But he used his good looks in order to give pleasure to other guys. Letting them do whatever they wanted felt good – in the short term, at least.

Being pleased? That was harder. If he wasn't giving Jackson pleasure, what was he giving him? Was this pity? Was he being used somehow? Was he expected to romance him, to be his Noah now that he'd seen Cam happy settling down with Noah? *Could* he be that kind of guy for Jackson?

He didn't want to think about the implications of this realization, but it stayed on his mind. TV just wasn't enough to get his mind off it.

Chase made himself wait one more beer before headed to the gay bar.

Chase wasn't ashamed of going home with Antonio when they ran into each other again. The guy had been good enough last time. Under the heat of the dance floor, Antonio whispered filthy things about getting *him* off this time, too.

The thought both scared and pleased Chase. He kind of liked being made to shut up and feel good for ten seconds before his anxieties kicked back in again. More importantly, he wanted to get fucked, and Antonio would give him that much.

Antonio's car was parked in a different lot this time, behind a commercial building. It was a bit of a shorter walk and more private anyway.

This time, Chase rolled over onto his front when he slid into the backseat.

The weight of Antonio blanketed him. He let out a breath, wishing Antonio were just a little heavier and stronger... more muscled, like Jackson--

Oh, fuck. Don't think about him every time you hook up from now on...

Chase tried to focus on the here and now: the man who was grinding against his ass. His hard cock throbbed between them as he mouthed at the back of Chase's neck.

Something didn't feel right, but he quashed his gut instinct. His gut instinct had led him far fucking astray before, after all. The only way he'd know whether his intuition was right or not was to test it, and he was going to do that. Antonio probably didn't care why he got to fuck Chase again.

Antonio reached under him, squeezing his cock and rubbing sensually. He ran his other hand up across Chase's stomach.

Chase moaned, pressing his forehead hard into the seat. Antonio's hands wandered south to unfasten his jeans and slide them down. Again, Chase fingered himself briefly. Then, Antonio unzipped his own pants and a condom packet crackled in the silence of the car.

Antonio's cock pressed against his opening. Chase breathed out, curling his fingers into the seat. At least his partner took it slowly and let the lubricant from the condom ease him inside instead of pushing it.

"You are all right?"

"I'm good," Chase answered breathily, his thighs shaking. "Thanks."

As Antonio slid into him, Chase pressed his forehead down and arched his hips more. He was going to have reddened grid lines from the seat across his forehead after this, but he didn't care.

"You are hot again," Antonio observed. "I'm glad you came back."

Chase moaned in response. Honestly, he couldn't say the same. He hadn't been looking for Antonio until they bumped into each other while dancing.

Antonio fucked him slower this time for the first couple of minutes.The car bounced with the force of Antonio's thrusts. The Italian student grunted as he pounded into Chase. Chase's cock throbbed with need under him. Chase slid his hand under himself to jerk himself off fast and hard.

The air was hot in here. The night absolutely silent besides the rough slaps of skin on skin, the grunts and moans, and the roughness of their breathing.

"Let me please you."

Chase let go of his cock and grabbed the seat instead, breathing out a quiet, "Hah! Ahh..." when that firm hand wrapped around him and started to jerk him off.

The rough, tight ring of fingers sliding down his shaft alternated with sharp thrusts into him and across the sensitive prostate...

Chase lost himself in the moment until his body started to tighten with involuntary pleasure. "Yes...!" He heaved himself up to slide his arm under himself again and try to keep his hand over the tip of his cock.

"Come," Antonio breathed out huskily, emphasizing it with a sharper thrust of his hips.

The throb through his prostate made his cock stiffen further. His body was tense, his stomach pulled tight, his thighs quivered... And then, he spilled over the edge fast and hard. It was blindingly hard, but over quickly.

When the momentary blissful black faded, Chase's chest heaved. He'd squeezed Antonio hard, clenching and milking him. All the while, Antonio kept fucking however and whenever he could.

Antonio was coming, too, with unmistakable shuddery thrusts and grunts.

When Antonio's hips slowed and he pulled his cock out, Chase lay still. He let him scoot back out of the car first again.

Chase yanked up his jeans and rolled onto his back. He sat up to scoot out of the car.

Antonio leaned against the door, giving him a hand up by gripping his bicep and pulling him upright. He let go as soon as Chase was on his feet. "You going home?"

Chase dusted himself off and stepped back. "Yeah."

"I could drive you."

Chase shook his head. "I like to walk." When Antonio leaned in to kiss his cheeks again, he turned his face away and clapped Antonio's shoulder again.

As he strode out of the parking lot, he heard Antonio's car start up and pull away in the opposite direction.

The sex hadn't been *bad*.

It had just been... nothing. Flat. Dull. Disappointing? Maybe a little.

His phone went off, and he pulled it out to idly glance at it, then swallowed hard.

Had a great time today. Off to bed but thinking of you. xx

For the first time in hours, his heart leapt into his throat with excitement. Even dancing hadn't thrilled him, but one lousy text felt like a double espresso in his veins. He reread it a few times, trying to come up with a reply that was sufficiently flirty, yet casual.

It had been months since Chase had felt that giddiness and his fingers tingled with excitement...

Me too. Sleep tight. Can't wait for tomorrow ;)

He stopped dead in the middle of the sidewalk as his fingers hovered over the "send" button.

"Oh, fuck. I really like him."

This meant the end of his hookups. It was pointless trying to fill the hole – in any sense of the word – with someone else when there was *one* guy he wanted. He wasn't stupid enough to keep trying anyway. One fuck with Antonio had been enough to tell him that much.

Chase pressed "send" and pocketed his phone for the walk home.

Nineteen

JACKSON

"So then, the guy decided he didn't really *want* a dragon tattoo anyway, and he told me he'd come back later. Floyd said he comes in about once a month to look at getting something but he never actually does."

Jackson's eyes and focus were on the billet he was forging into the sword. From tang to tip, it took a tremendous amount of work to keep the blade straight yet flexible, strong yet beautiful. Knowing Chase wasn't going to use it for actual fighting, he could have just joined a few pieces of metal.

But Chase deserved something beautiful through and through, not just skin-deep.

"When he called in this morning, I told him he's got to put a deposit down before I sketch anything. Well, he didn't like that. When he threatened to go to another shop, I told him he could if he wanted. But I've got a lot more experience, and he'll get what he pays for."

"Jesus. Damn straight," Jackson agreed, letting out a breath as he carried the billet back to the fire. His t-shirt sleeves were pushed up to bare his shoulders. He'd left the door to the workshop open to try to vent a little of the hot air in here. Even though it was evening, they were having a heat wave – perhaps the last one of the season – and it was at least thirty degrees inside, like a hot Canadian summer day.

It was going to take so long to finish the sword. It took a long time to forge the blade itself, and there was the detail he wanted to put into the hilt and grip, the tempering process... but Chase was also planning an elaborate piece for him.

And having Chase's company in the workshop was wonderful. Chase wouldn't stop talking, which was fine by Jackson. He liked the background noise of his work, but human company was so much better.

"So I'll keep you updated if he calls back tomorrow," Chase concluded with a laugh. He fidgeted with his sleeves as he sat on the workbench next to Jackson. He was much less afraid of the sparks and noise now; he even handed over tools now and then. And he didn't seem to mind the heat at all.

"This sounds very dramatic," Jackson teased.

"It's about as dramatic as it gets. Except when parents come in to get their kids tattooed and yell at us about how we should let them..."

Jackson's eyebrows shot up. "Oh. Wow."

"I've dealt with a bunch of those before. Luckily Floyd has a no-under-18s policy across the whole shop. Another one I was freelancing from let individual artists decide, and that was a fuckin' mess."

Jackson clamped his tongs around the blade and started to hammer out another few inches of blade. Molding the glowing, white-hot metal into something new would never, ever get old for him. Making weapons out of it was just *cool*.

Once he was done that series of blows, Jackson breathed out and went to dunk it in a barrel of water and cool it off.

"Did you decide what you're thinking for the grip yet?"

"I like the first design you showed me."

Jackson grinned. He prided himself on getting a quick sense of each client's style and aesthetic preferences. He'd called Chase's perfectly. It was easy to see what he liked from his tattoo style anyway. "Great."

"Sooo, you said you were cool with a tattoo design up to three inches, right?"

"Mmhmm?" Jackson suspected he knew where this was going.

"Well... have you thought about anything bigger?"

Jackson grinned. "Now and then. You wanna do a full sleeve or something?"

"Not if you don't want it," Chase laughed. "But, you know, a little bigger would look just fine on you. You're tall and broad enough. All that canvas..."

Jackson snorted with laughter. He carried the blade to the table to set down before he crashed on the bench next to Chase. He leaned back, stretching out his arms. "That just sounds kinda creepy. All this bare skin being a canvas."

"You know what I mean," Chase laughed. "Now you're the one making morbid jokes."

Jackson shrugged and leaned in to kiss Chase's cheek. "It's rubbing off on me. How you doing?"

Just as he'd thought, Chase hesitated to answer. "Oh... You know."

"You seem pretty worked up. Not that I mind you talking a lot, but..." Jackson trailed off. He turned to face Chase properly. Chase was in light jeans and a t-shirt again. Brave man, not to be wearing shorts in this heat. "You're not gonna faint, are you?"

Chase broke up laughing. "No. No," he repeated, reaching out to take Jackson's hand. He ran his hand up Jackson's bare arm to rub his back. Chase scooted a little closer on the bench. "I'm fine in here. Just a lot of stuff on my mind."

"Like what?"

"How much I wanna kiss you when you're swinging that hammer and sparks are flying and the forge is roaring..." Chase leaned in and up. By the last word, his lips pressed against Jackson's.

Jackson wrapped his arm around Chase's shoulders to pull him in for a good, sloppy kiss, their lips open. Chase's hand running up from his knee to his hip was *very* distracting as Jackson pressed into the kiss with a moan.

Jesus, Chase got to him fast. His cock was already hardening as Chase's hand caressed his hip and outer thigh. It wandered across to the top of his thigh as Chase sucked Jackson's lower lip between his own.

Jackson *wanted* Chase. It was so easy to want him. The way Chase moved, spoke, watched, flirted... and most of all, kissed...

He pulled back from the kiss, his chest heaving for breath. It was so fucking hot in here that *he* might just faint, especially if they were going to have sex.

"Wanna go inside?"

"Oh, God, yes," Chase admitted.

Jackson laughed. "Let me just cool off the forge. It'll be a few minutes."

Chase's voice was low and suggestive, sending a shiver straight down Jackson's spine. "I can think of *plenty* of ways to fill a few minutes."

It was so hard to pull away from Chase's arm around his back and Chase's hand rubbing his knee. Jackson hauled himself to his feet. Chase stood up, too, lingering by the work bench while Jackson raked out the coals and watered them down.

He *could* head straight inside, but he made a policy of never, ever leaving without checking that the coals were cool. Embers could burn for hours, spark up again, and start a fire.

Christ, the fire under his skin was almost impossible to bear.

"I'm just *waiting* to be kissed over here," Chase murmured.

When Jackson glanced back at him, Chase was sitting on the worktable, his knees apart. He kicked his feet in the air and braced his hands behind himself.

"You're so fucking gorgeous." Jackson shook his head. He set down his water pail and strode toward Chase.

Chase was already flushed from the heat and it was impossible to tell if he was blushing, but he smiled and winked. "So are you, Hottie McBlacksmith, handling your rods..."

He spent a moment trying to fight the urge to say it. He lost the battle. "That was actually a billet."

Chase pouted, his long eyelashes fluttering closed for a second as he rolled his head back in a quiet lament. "Not the moment."

Jackson sidled up between Chase's knees. He braced his hands on either side of Chase and leaned in to press his lips to Chase's now-exposed throat. Chase's Adam's apple bobbed as he murmured against bare skin, "Sorry... not sorry."

Chase murmured, "You got anything else you wanna teach me?"

"I'm sure I'll think of something." Jackson had so many ideas, and none of them were appropriate for his workspace.

Chase squeezed Jackson's hips between his knees and flung his arms around his neck. He leaned up for a few more slow, lazy kisses to fill the minutes while the coals burnt out.

Taking it slow didn't mean there wasn't chemistry crackling to life. It blazed through Jackson's chest and warmed his fingers. His toes curled into his work boots and his heart pounded with pure need...

Jackson pulled back and whispered, "It's been long enough." Chase let go of him and he stepped away. He offered him a hand to help him slide off the table and onto his feet again.

They walked hand-in-hand out of the workshop as Jackson locked it up behind him. He led him through the grass toward the back door.

Once they were inside with their shoes off, Jackson stopped in the kitchen. They needed water after all that heat.

Chase leaned on the counter. That little frown line was back between Chase's eyebrows. His gaze kept flickering around the living room.

Jackson had to ask. "What's on your mind?"

Chase gulped down the rest of his glass of water, slid it back, and looked evenly at Jackson. "Are you saving it 'til marriage?"

The solemn question made Jackson burst out laughing. "Wait – no. What? No..."

Chase cracked a little smile of relief now. "I just... we've messed around but we haven't fucked, you know?"

"Blowjobs still count as sex," Jackson idly pointed out, but he saw what Chase meant. He put their glasses in the sink and came around the counter to lean next to Chase. Their gazes were locked.

Chase reached out to press a hand against Jackson's chest. He ran his hand up to his shoulder and fidgeted with a bit of his hair. "So what's holding you back?"

"Nothing," Jackson honestly admitted. "I feel like we're clicking really well--"

"You think?" Chase grinned.

"I just didn't want you to think I only wanted sex. You're worth more than that."

Chase paused. He started to smile. "Yeah?"

He's precious. Jackson leaned in to kiss him once, then murmured, "Yeah."

"Thank you. Take me to bed?" Chase's voice was soft and hopeful. He was watching Jackson like he couldn't believe his luck.

Jackson felt exactly the same. He took Chase's hand to lead him through the kitchen and living room and up the stairs. Every few steps, they paused to kiss each other. They chuckled, then laughed against each other's lips. It was somehow funny even though there was nothing to really laugh at.

They reached Jackson's bedroom door. Chase grabbed Jackson's hand to hold him back for a moment. Jackson tilted his head curiously.

Chase murmured, "I've already said I like you... but I really do."

Jackson swallowed hard as his heart soared. Chase was sweet, wickedly funny, clever, and right now, his heart was bared.

He turned toward Chase and reached out to tip his chin up with his thumb. He pressed a kiss against the man's lips.

"I really like you, too," he assured Chase.

Chase grinned and grabbed Jackson's hand to pull him into the bedroom.

Jackson flicked on the bedside lamp with the wall switch, and Chase was already kissing him hard. His hands closed around Chase's slender waist to pull him in. He kissed him right back, running his hand up along Chase's spine to the back of his neck.

Chase slid his leg between Jackson's so he could grind against his hip. His arms were around Jackson's neck again.

Jackson gently steered Chase backward toward the bed, kissing him for each step he took. By the time Chase flopped onto his back on the bed, Chase's eyes sparkled with laughter.

"What?" Jackson grinned.

"You're cheesy as fuck."

Jackson smirked. "I get the impression you *like* cheesy as fuck."

"Damn it." Chase sighed dramatically, unbuttoning his shirt. "I can't help it."

Jackson winked and leaned in to kiss Chase's neck and the hollow of his throat. With each button unfastened, he kissed a little further toward his soft belly. He mouthed at Chase's hipbone and flicked his tongue along the waistband. Then, he kissed back up over his stomach and chest.

"Oh, fuck, that's right. You're a tease."

Jackson snickered. He started to suck on Chase's skin. He found a spot that made Chase almost convulse with pleasure just below his ribcage. "I don't remember you complaining..." He sucked just a little higher. "...when you came in my mouth..." He pressed an open-mouthed kiss across Chase's nipple. "...whimpering and thrusting all the while..."

Chase turned red and mumbled something, his neck and ears flushing with his blush. Holy crap, he was adorable.

Chase was already so fucking hard – the tent was easy to see pressing against his jeans. It was so tempting just to make him come undone yet again under his mouth. But Chase wanted more than a blowjob today, and so did Jackson. `

Jackson flicked his tongue a few more times across Chase's nipple, still kissing open-mouthed to warm his skin. In response, Chase's breath caught again. His body pressed up into Jackson's as he straddled Jackson's hip from below. His hips rotated in a slow, needy circle, his cock rubbing against Jackson's hip...

Jackson moved his kisses up to kiss around the tattoo. "It still has sensation there, right?"

"Yes," Chase snorted in momentary laughter. "There's no difference."

"I haven't even gotten one!" Jackson reminded Chase, laughing before pressing a few kisses to the muscle between his shoulder and neck. "Don't make fun of me."

"If you make fun of me for calling them rods and not... bouillon..."

It was Jackson's turn to choke back a laugh. "Billets."

"Billets... Anyway, shut up and get your shirt off."

Jackson laughed again as Chase's fingers curled around the hem and yanked the light fabric up over his head. Chase tossed his shirt aside, then reached down to fumble at their waists and unfasten jeans.

Jackson almost tore Chase's jeans open, yanking them down and off as he scooted down the bed. He helped Chase kick them off and pulled off his socks. Chase's half-hard cock sprang free, eagerly awaiting his attention.

First, Jackson knelt back on his heels to admire him.

Shit, he was even more gorgeous now that he could see all his tattoos. There were sleeves of elegant animals twining around his biceps and forearms and the clock tattoo above his heart, of course. But there were more. Just below his waistband were three feathered silhouettes of birds with roughly feathered and faded wings and tails. Along his legs, he had gorgeous stenciled geometric patterns. They faded into roses with thorns, much like his wrists, along his thighs.

There was still plenty of bare skin along his legs, chest, stomach, and shoulders, though. How much did he plan to fill in?

"Most of my portfolio is written on me."

Jackson dragged his eyes away from the shades and colors of the tattoos crisscrossing Chase's skin. "I'd hire you," Jackson teased. He knelt upright to slide his jeans down, too.

"I'd let you," Chase countered. "Look at all that canvas! I keep saying you should do more with it."

Jackson grinned as he tossed aside his own jeans and crawled back up over Chase to kiss him. "We'll see," he murmured.

"Is that a maybe?"

"That's a we'll-see," Jackson laughed. "Hold on." He leaned over to grab a condom and lube.

"But I'm so kissable and I'm not being kissed, *again*."

Jackson swooped back down to press his lips hard against Chase's. Their bare skin radiated and doubled the heat for each of them as their bodies nestled against each other's. As they kissed, their cocks slotted together between their stomachs. Jackson ground down against Chase hard to make the most of it.

Chase moaned into his mouth, his head rolling back as his eyes slid closed. Jackson kissed him two or three more times for good measure, gasping for breath between kisses. He fumbled to open the lube and get it across his fingers.

"You're gonna finger me?"

"Do you want me too?"

Chase nodded hard. His eyes were open again, fixed on Jackson with fascination. "I love it," he whispered. "I'm pretty squirmy..."

"Let me discover that on my own," Jackson chided with a wink. He slid his fingers between the cheeks to find the opening. His fingertips danced around it first in small swirls. Chase exhaled quickly and pulled his knees further apart and up.

Jackson turned his head and kissed Chase's knee as he slid two fingertips inside the opening. He took it good and slow at first.

"Hnnh," Chase moaned quietly, his own nails digging into his shins. "Yes..."

Jackson let his fingers slide further into the warm tightness, pushing them up into him. As Chase gasped for breath, Jackson curled them to lightly stroke along the little bump. His eyes were fixed on Chase's expressions.

Chase's face showed them all: discomfort for a few seconds, then relief, then pleasure and outright joy. "Ohhh, yes," Chase groaned.

"You *do* like that," Jackson smirked, fucking him good and slow with two fingers at first. Every time he pushed them up inside Chase and rubbed that bump with the pads of his fingers, Chase's body quivered. He tried to push harder into Jackson's fingers.

Chase's breathing was quick, his flushed lips parted as his cheeks burned with pleasure. "Yes," Chase whispered now and then. "More...! Christ, you can give me more..."

Every time he swore, especially invoking God or Christ or hell, he said them with a glint in his eye. It was like he wasn't just emptily repeating bad words. Chase seemed to *mean* every curse, which made his vocal reactions a thousand times hotter.

Chase's arousal, the way he spat his words like he dared Jackson to defy them, was the hottest thing. He wanted to encourage it.

Chase wanted more? Jackson would give him more.

He added a third finger, sliding it inside to rub firmly across the prostate. He went up and down, over and over, crooking his fingers just right until Chase's back arched and his thighs started to tremble.

"Jesus. Jackson, don't – don't make me come yet...!"

Jackson grinned. He jerked Chase's cock a few times in his other hand before reluctantly sliding his fingers free from Chase's body. "You *are* fuckin' squirmy. I love how vocal you are."

Chase peeked through his lashes, and Jackson leaned down to peck his lips again. Once the condom was on, he stroked himself for Chase's viewing pleasure.

"Smoking hot."

Jackson grinned, scooting close to blanket Chase with his weight. He rubbed the tip of his cock in the crack and around the opening. He was always willing to tease Chase just a little more.

"Please...!" Chase moaned, raising one leg to slide around Jackson's waist.

Jackson pushed into the warmth and tightness of Chase. He breathed out a moan of relief at the same moment Chase groaned. God, he'd been imagining this for days – ever since he'd first kissed Chase.

"Oh, yes," Chase murmured, and Jackson smiled. Their nipples brushed as Jackson's body slid back and forth across Chase's. He thrust slowly at first, keeping his weight braced on one forearm above Chase's head. When Chase started to push into him in a silent demand for more, he sped up his pace gradually.

One thrust at a time, Chase started to melt under him, his lips parting as his eyes grew hazy.

"I love the looks on your face," Jackson whispered and kissed Chase. Chase tried to return the kiss, but Jackson wanted to overwhelm him with pleasure. He kept sneaking kisses at Chase's lips and little sucks of the tip of his tongue or one of his lips.

"Y-You're... fuck," Chase moaned, a quick smile flickering across his face. He wrapped his arms around Jackson's back and clenched around him. "Christ, you're big. And good... and big."

Who wouldn't like hearing that? Jackson grinned and mouthed at Chase's neck and over to his ear. "And you're *perfect*," he whispered, then sucked on Chase's earlobe.

Chase whimpered and clenched around him. Ripples ran through the muscles of his thighs and stomach as his back arched.

"You're so sensitive..." Jackson added wonderingly. He flicked his tongue along the rim before pressing an open-mouthed kiss behind Chase's ear.

"You can leave hickeys if you want."

"Yeah?" Jackson kissed under Chase's ear until he found a spot that made Chase's breath catch and his nails dig into Jackson's back.

He kissed hard and sucked against the skin, playing his tongue along the sensitive flesh. A full-throated groan of pleasure slipped from Chase's throat. "Yes...! Yes, baby, yes... oh, fuck..."

Jackson sucked firmly for a few moments more before kissing gently across that spot. "So grown-up," he teased. "Showing up to work with hickeys..."

"Fuck off."

Jackson smirked. "Not that I mind claiming you..."

It was getting almost painful to stay slow and deep. He needed to go harder – wanted to fuck Chase into the mattress until Chase was crying out in constant, over-whelming pleasure...

Jackson pushed his hips against Chase's faster and harder now. His well-honed muscles flexed to drive his hardened dick straight into Chase's needy hole. Every thrust of his cock head across the throbbing prostate inside made Chase's body seize up and a quiet grunt escape from his throat.

Chase gasped and his nails dug hard into Jackson's back. "Like – like *that*! Oh, God, yes...!"

Jackson was *so* happy to deliver what Chase wanted. He grunted, then groaned as Chase pulled him down enough to breathlessly kiss his lips. Their bodies drove together, and Chase grunted again, then another time.

That was the hardest and deepest he could drive himself, and just about as fast as he dared to go. Chase was coming undone under the attention.

"Yes...! Please, oh, Jackson, fuck... yes, like that... yes...!"

Chase's thighs were spasming and quivering now. His stomach tensed and his expression tautened with that same pleasure. He couldn't kiss Jackson now, his mouth falling open as he gasped for breath. He was so fucking *beautiful* Jackson almost couldn't stand it.

"Come for me, Chase. I can feel every bone in your body

wanting to," Jackson moaned into Chase's ear. He kissed along his jaw and neck again. He sucked on Chase's neck as he tweaked Chase's nipple.

"*Yes!*" Chase grunted, grinding his hard cock between their bodies with each hard thrust. "Yes... yes..." He could barely seem to breathe, and Jackson fucking loved having so much effect on him.

His body was tightening again, and Jackson felt like perhaps this was the final moment...

It was.

Chase clenched hard around him and arched clear off the bed. His cock, trapped between their bodies, squirted hard, fast jets of passion between their stomachs. Chase's head rolled back. "Yes...! Jackson!" he moaned one last time. He subsided into a series of grunts, whimpers, and precious, fucking *hot* moans. His body clenched and quivered and writhed against the sheets.

His tightness milked Jackson's throbbing cock until Jackson felt his own balls draw tight. That was all the warning he had.

"Christ!" Jackson gasped at how fast and hard it was about to hit him, then stifled his moan in Chase's neck. He buried his face in Chase's shoulder as his cock plunged deep within Chase. It pulsed its own stream of wet pleasure with each unconscious, relentless thrust of his hips.

"Oh, God, yes," Chase gasped. "Come, Jackson. That's it, baby. Fuck, you're so good... so good..." His hands ran up and down Jackson's back. The extra stimulation overloaded Jackson's nerves in the most pleasurable ways.

"Ohhh," Jackson groaned. He slowed and stopped thrusting once he felt the last few drops trickle out. His cock started to twitch and soften again. He pulled gently out of Chase but stayed blanketing him with his weight.

Chase turned his head to kiss Jackson a few times as Jackson tried to catch his breath.

His head spun. All he could still feel or hear or see was the beautiful, tattooed man writhing under him. Chase let him hear every single second of pleasure that had raced through him.

As if Jackson hadn't known already, this wasn't just a passing fancy. He had utterly fallen for Chase, and his heart clenched with worry about how Chase was going to react to his next suggestion.

He rolled onto his side and cuddled into Chase, not even bothering to take off the condom just yet. He was too interested in running his hand up along that smooth chest to caress Chase's cheek.

"Hi." Chase cupped his cheek in return. Those eyes that had been hazy and distant were bright with pleasure and interest again.

Jackson smiled. Chase had such a beautiful little sense of humor. "Hi," he answered.

"You're about ten times sexier than I imagined, and believe me... it was pretty hot in my shower already."

Jackson burst out laughing now. "I... Thank you."

"You're welcome." Chase winked. "It'll be even hotter now, though."

Jackson roughly pulled Chase against him to hug him, rolling onto his back so Chase lay against his chest. He didn't give a fuck that they needed to wash up sooner or later... this was more important.

Chase easily moved with him and flopped along him. He pressed his cheek into Jackson's shoulder and hugged around his shoulders as much as he could. Jackson gently kissed him, and Chase lifted his head to return the kiss.

"You are *so goddamn beautiful,*" Jackson murmured. "Sorry, I know I keep saying it, but... I just wanna make sure you know."

This time, instead of the flippant acceptance, Chase gazed into Jackson's eyes, and... were his eyes a little wetter than normal? *Oh, shit. No... wait. He's not crying. Phew.*

Chase blinked and shook his head, a fond smile on his lips. "Thank you. I don't usually hear that *after* sex."

"Well, I mean it," Jackson murmured. "Any man would be lucky to have you."

There it was again: the nervousness, like a skittish animal in his arms. Chase didn't pull away or run, though. He just paused, then settled against Jackson. "I wanted to talk about that."

"Mmhmm?" Jackson carded his fingers through Chase's hair, waiting to see what he had to say.

Chase winced. "This probably isn't the moment," he murmured, "but I wanted to tell you: I hooked up with some guy at a bar yesterday."

Ouch. Jackson swallowed hard but tried to reserve his judgment instead of leaping to conclusions like he always did. If he had one fault, it was hotheadedness, and he wasn't going to let it fuck up a promising relationship.

They weren't exclusive. Therefore, no fault.

"Okay."

Chase breathed out a sigh, relaxing when Jackson didn't snap at him. "It... it didn't go too well. I realized I can't... I don't *want* to... just hook up anymore. I don't want just any guy around."

Was he saying what Jackson hoped...?

Jackson swallowed hard, resisting the urge to cross his fingers. "So?" he asked, letting Chase tell him instead of assuming.

"So I want to... to date you. Just you."

Oh my God. Jackson grinned. He knew his face gave away his answer already, but he couldn't change *that* much of himself. Open book or not, Chase seemed to like that about him. "Really?"

Chase smiled sheepishly. "Yeah."

"All it took was one douche? I hope he wasn't too much of a douche. I can go intimidate him."

Chase laughed and shook his head. "I don't give a crap about him. It just helped me realize that I wanna try dating you. I haven't dated anyone in a while, so I might be really bad at being a boyfriend, but..."

"That's fine," Jackson assured him. "I haven't, either. I don't think there's any rulebook."

"Good. I'm bad at rules."

Jackson smirked and kissed Chase. "Hi, then, boyfriend."

He wished he could have photographed the look of joy that spread across Chase's face. "Hi." Chase was clearly trying not to be too enthusiastic and it was utterly failing. It made Jackson laugh.

"Wha'?"

"Nothing," Jackson chuckled, caressing Chase's cheek.

"I – I should head home for the night, though. I got work early tomorrow... and all week. And I should go to fencing, since I'm paying for classes, for some reason," Chase laughed.

Jackson groaned. "Classes *and* more overtime?"

"Yeah," Chase mumbled, sighing as he kissed Jackson once more. "But I can show off my hickey to everyone."

Jackson smirked. "You can leave some for me, too, sometime."

"I will," Chase winked.

He has to get up and go now, Jackson reminded himself. Of course, the logical thing to do was kiss him so well that he'd forget he had to leave.

Chase's lips caressed his own as Chase's lashes flickered closed and their noses bumped. Though Jackson was cooling off now, the warmth of Chase's slight body against his own was a treat.

This was his favorite part, and it looked like Chase wasn't opposed to it, either.

Minutes later, their hands in each other's hair and lips still brushing gently, Chase groaned. "Okay, I *really* gotta go."

Jackson snickered. "Fine," he murmured and kissed Chase just once more before letting go of him.

There was a companionable silence between them now. They cleaned up and dressed, still touching and kissing at every opportunity.

"I think you're trying to lure me into staying here," Chase finally accused him. He was beaming as he leaned into Jackson while they stood in the middle of the bedroom.

Jackson wrapped his arms around Chase's waist to sway lightly with him. He was lovely to hug. "Maybe."

"S'not gonna work this time. Maybe next time."

"Okay." Jackson kissed the back of Chase's neck and let go, then reached out to open the door for him. "I'll keep trying."

Chase's laughs were lighthearted now, his smile bright. He sauntered downstairs, followed by Jackson, to collect his shoes at the door.

Then, Chase reached out to grab Jackson's t-shirt and pull

him in for one more good, slow kiss. "I'll see you soon, hm? After this week."

"God, that'll feel like forever," Jackson lamented. He hugged Chase close and kissed him back. "Whenever you're free."

"Soon as I *can* be free," Chase promised, his voice so sincere. "And Jackson?"

"Yeah?"

"Thanks for being so patient with me." Chase's gaze flickered between Jackson's eyes, some unguarded emotion on his face that Jackson couldn't place yet.

Jackson just wanted to pull him in for another rough hug. Whatever was on Chase's mind, he'd learn it someday and it would no doubt make him angry. Instead, for now, he ran his hand back through Chase's hair affectionately. "No problem. That's what boyfriends are for, huh?"

The moment he heard the word, Chase grinned again. "Yeah," he agreed. He leaned in for one more peck before he pulled open the door. "See you, Jackson."

"Bye." Jackson leaned in the door, watching Chase walk down the path to the sidewalk. He leaned his head against the edge of the open door, pleasure still thrumming through his body.

I have a boyfriend. And not just any boyfriend... Chase.

There were no words to describe the sense of rightness that had settled deep into his bones.

Twenty

CHASE

"You have a *boyfriend* now? Shit, Chase. Why didn't you tell me?"

Chase sprayed glass cleaner on the cloth, ducking his head as he blushed. He glanced at Floyd as he wiped in circles along the cabinet. His boss was about to leave for the day and had asked about his plans tonight. He'd subtly dropped the hint that he had *plans*.

"You were away at the Maritime tattoo show, and we were busy today..."

"Aw, man, that's awesome. Who is it? Do I know him?"

"I dunno. Jackson Riley. He's a blacksmith."

"Yeah, I think I've heard the name... I don't know him though," Floyd shook his head. "You're growing up now."

"Growing up?"

"You know, it's not all about bars. Everyone's gotta settle down sooner or later, gay or straight."

Chase frowned. He didn't especially like the implications. *Yeah, I hook up a lot, but not because I'm gay...* He let it go, though. "Yeah."

Floyd winced. "And I just stacked all that overtime on you. Sorry."

"Hey, the paycheck's nice," Chase laughed. "But yeah, it's our first date since we got together. We've both been working overtime..."

Floyd shook his head as he patted down his pockets for his car keys. "Let me know how it goes, huh? I wanna meet this guy if you get serious."

"I will."

"Call me if you need anything." Floyd raised a hand and waved.

"I'll be fine."

Once he was alone in the shop, Chase put away the glass cleaner and pulled out his phone. He didn't make a habit of slacking off work – even when Floyd said it was okay – but he had some important tasks.

Like finding a new apartment.

Chase still didn't know how his family had found this address – or even figured out that he'd come to Fredericton. He'd only told a few friends back at home in Ontario where he was going. None of them would have leaked it.

As he scrolled through Kijiji on his phone, he opened a few places in new tabs to check them out. At least there was a lot on the market thanks to the students moving at the end of the summer.

He didn't even notice the door open until he heard it jingle and slipped his phone under the counter. "Hey..."

Oh, wow. This guy was gorgeous.

"Uh, hi. Can I help you?"

The stranger's soft brown eyes were already fixed on him as he strode up to the counter. He was perhaps in his mid-twenties or even early thirties, with dark stubble. "Hello. I'm Alex. You're Chase, aren't you?"

Chase was wary. This man already knew him. "I am." His hand slipped to the baseball bat beneath the counter. "Why?"

"I'm here to... confess, I suppose." The stranger's voice was soft, yet clear. He wore a troubled frown as he rested his hands on the counter, directly watching Chase. "I'm a private investigator here in Fredericton. Your parents hired me to look into your whereabouts."

They did what? Chase's jaw dropped.

"I'm normally never allowed to break the rules like this and... betray my client's confidentiality..." Alex trailed off. "But this case was a little different. I couldn't just not tell you."

"That you were spying on me?"

What was his life? Who the hell had spies sent after them except... mafia guys and, like, gang members?

"Yes, if you want to put it like that. I haven't been watching your every movement, if that helps. I know it doesn't."

Chase was pale. He let go of the bat and gripped the counter. Hard. "It doesn't."

"I gave them your home address before I knew what was going on. They... let a hint slip about why they needed it... and I ended our working relationship. They don't know your workplace or new name."

"Are they coming for me?"

Alex winced, his gaze flickering up to the camera and back at Chase. Then, he squared his shoulders against the consequences of his answer. "Yes."

"Wh-When? Who?"

"I don't know—"

"Fat lot of good you are, investigator."

Alex sighed. He wasn't trying to argue this one. He knew he'd fucked up in whatever moral compass he had. "I suspect it will take a few more days to arrange a trip out here, especially if they're driving. They didn't say."

"Are you here to help me go undercover or... what?" Chase snapped. "Just assuage your guilty conscience and feel better about yourself? Leave me to deal with it?" Chase's demands grew louder.

"I... I wish I'd known what I do now. When I asked their reasons, they lied, and I didn't question it. I'm truly sorry, for whatever that's worth." Alex raised his hands and stepped back from the counter. "I'd suggest moving, though that's not always practical."

"Already on it, genius." Chase pulled his phone out from under the counter.

Alex sighed. He drew a card out of his pocket and slid it across the counter. "Look, if you need help, let me know anytime. I'm sorry for what's happened. I owe you a few."

"In case *I* want to spy on people here," Chase snorted. "Very helpful."

Alex watched him for a few moments, and Chase *hated* the sympathy in his expression. It was all too familiar. When they found out, everyone just fucking felt sorry for him instead of doing anything helpful. "You can call me anytime. Good luck."

As the door rattled shut behind him, Chase let out a slow breath and thumped his head on the counter. Much as he wanted to tear up the card, he didn't. He just slid it into his pocket for later.

Fuck. His parents knew where he lived, but at least no more than that.

Eventually, he straightened up again. He shouldn't have taken it all out on Alex, but finally, he'd met someone he could blame for his current situation. Moving was expensive and shitty and a hassle and now unavoidable.

Asshole.

"I haven't been watching your every movement," Chase muttered sarcastically. "Wonderful. At least they can't find me when I'm not home. Fuck."

Movement outside the shop window made him startle, his breath catching in his throat.

It was Jackson.

Chase enjoyed watching his boyfriend squint at the sign to make sure he had the right place before pulling open the tattoo shop door. "Hey, good-looking."

Jackson laughed as the door swung shut and he crossed the shop floor in a few strides. "Hello yourself, gorgeous."

"I still have half an hour left." Chase leaned over the counter for a kiss. "Are you cool hanging out here?"

"Yeah, of course. I came early to watch you work, if that's okay."

"It's not very interesting. I have one appointment to finish touching up a tattoo in a couple minutes." Chase checked his phone for the time. "Other than that, nothing booked."

Jackson smiled. "I'll just talk, then." He dragged a chair from the waiting area over to the counter. He plopped himself down on it, stretching out his legs. "How was your day?"

I can't tell him about all this shit yet... Chase glanced across the shop and nodded. "It was all right. It was a day."

"Been a long week."

"Yeah? Your staircases are all done?"

"Thank *God*," Jackson groaned emphatically. He rubbed

his hands down his face, stretching out his cheeks. "Bleeergh."

Chase laughed, propping his chin on his fist and his elbow on the counter. "Yeah? At least all that's done. I told Floyd I've got a boyfriend now..."

"Yeah?" Jackson's switch from melancholy to excitement was instant. He straightened up and folded his hands in his lap in a clear effort to calm down. "Cool."

Seeing someone his size get excited about everything was so cute. Chase smirked. "Yeah, and he shouldn't give me as much overtime now. That was the last show of the season anyway."

The door rattled and swung open as his client entered. She needed a few more details in her flower watercolor tattoo, and Chase was excited to finish it off. "Hey, Kate. How's it goin'?"

"Great. You? Sorry, am I early or late?"

"I'm good. No, that's just my boyfriend," Chase grinned. "He wanted to hang out and watch me work."

"You wanna watch Chase finish my tattoo?" Kate offered, already turning to show off the work in progress splashed across her upper arm. It was just about done, except for some light outlines they'd both agreed the flower's center needed and a few more splashes of color to even it out.

Jackson's eyebrows raised. "Oh, you don't mind? Yeah, I'd love that. I've never seen one."

"Man, by your fourth or fifth it'll get old," Kate laughed.

Chase led them both to the back room he'd already set up. He pulled up a chair for Jackson, hummed, and slipped on gloves. "So, just like we agreed on?"

"Yeah," Kate nodded. "I can't wait to see it."

"Me neither. I think it'll come out great with just a bit

more detail." Chase had already set up his needle, so he connected the gun to the machine and tested it to make sure it vibrated. He was using a shader rather than a liner for softer lines. Then he'd have to switch to color to blend in the final colors around the edge of the tattoo.

As soon as her skin was wiped down, his gloves changed, and the light on, Chase's focus was absolute.

His foot on the pedal, his pinky balanced his hand steadily on her skin. The needle vibrated and thrummed through his hand...

He carefully wiped away excess ink as he went. He was even more focused than usual from nervousness at being watched.

It wasn't like he'd never been watched before. It happened all the time. Bosses, apprentices, teachers, customers' partners...

But Jackson was different.

Chase drew a breath as he lifted his foot from the pedal and pulled the needle away. He smoothed a layer of Vaseline across her skin. "Now for the colors."

"Oh, wow, that looks great already." Kate knew to look past the reddened skin at the quality of the lines. Chase was thrilled with how smoothly they'd come out.

"Yeah, that's definitely what it needed."

Jackson murmured, "Wow. I bet everyone asks, but doesn't it hurt? You're bleeding..."

"Only a bit," Kate answered. "Somewhere fleshy, it's just a bit like getting pinched a lot. You sort of tune it out. My shoulder blade was the worst one – everything else was easy."

"Everyone's different," Chase added as he swapped

machines. He showed her the color he'd already added. "Just like we said, yeah?"

"If you're sure it'll come out right."

"I promise," Chase chuckled. It didn't always look the same in the bottle as on skin, after all.

"All right, go for it."

"You need a break first?"

"Nah, get 'er done."

Jackson laughed and settled back again, and Chase leaned in to start coloring. This was much more fun. He enjoyed sketching and shading in black ink, but clients always appreciated color. The extra pinks shading the edges of the flowers would make them stand out. Making it look like a watercolor was a thrilling challenge.

"How 'bout... that?" he murmured a few minutes later.

Jackson murmured, "Dude, that was cool."

Kate laughed at him, then turned to get a good look. "Ohhh, yeah. You were right. That *was* the right color." She examined it carefully. "Yeah, that's perfect. I think that's just what it needed."

"Great," Chase concluded. He glanced at Jackson. "That was a really simple session. Usually there's more back-and-forth or Sharpies..."

Kate added, "Fighting over color choices..."

Chase laughed. "I was right, though, huh?" he teased, flicking her shoulder gently. "Okay, I'll get that cleaned up and covered and you're on your way."

"Awesome. Thanks."

As Chase bandaged the spot, he felt Jackson watching him with admiration. It was hard not to grin.

Twenty-One

JACKSON

"MAN, THAT WAS COOL," JACKSON SAID FOR ABOUT THE THIRD time once Kate was out the door and it was back to the two of them. He had a vivid memory of Chase's hands so carefully working across bare skin. He was precise with the sharp instrument, millimeters at a time, to create permanent art.

Chase grinned. He acted embarrassed at the attention, but it was easy to tell he loved it. He checked his phone, then tossed it onto the counter and turned to the cash register. "You really liked watching that. Maybe you should get some yourself..."

Oh, he was incorrigible. Jackson just laughed. "Like I said, we're starting with one."

"It can be a bigger one..." Chase winked. He pulled out the cash drawer. "Wanna lock the door?"

Jackson strode to the door, and while he was at it, he turned the sign to read *Closed*. While Chase brought the drawer to the office and cleaned up the room, Jackson waited by the counter.

He wasn't a snoop, but sometimes he couldn't help but

notice things around him. His eyes were drawn down to the orange and beige of the Kijiji website on Chase's phone. It showed an apartment listing: one bedroom, one bathroom, close to downtown in Fredericton.

He's apartment-hunting? He never mentioned.

"You looking for a new place?" Jackson asked as soon as Chase emerged from the hall.

Chase almost froze on the spot. He gave a nervous smile and grabbed his phone to pocket it. "Yep."

That was weird. "Your lease coming up?"

"Uh, maybe, I dunno," Chase answered vaguely and patted his pockets down for his stuff. "Where we goin' for drinks?"

Jackson took the hint, as curious as he was about why he'd gotten that reaction. "C'mon, just in walking distance." After Chase locked up, Jackson took Chase's hand to walk down the street with him toward a bar. They could finally unwind and grab sandwiches, British-style chips, and a couple beers.

———

Jackson pushed back the empty basket of chips and wiped his fingers on a napkin, then hummed. "You never said why you're moving."

As much as he hated intruding on people's privacy, it was still bugging him. Chase's reaction was so weird – guilt, like he'd just been caught in the act of something or another.

Chase licked his lower lip and glanced down at his beer, his brow furrowed.

"I'm gonna ask what's going on when you act weird, you know," Jackson told him. "If you don't want me to know, you can tell me to fuck off. I won't be offended, I promise. You don't *have* to share everything with me."

Chase's shoulders sank and he offered Jackson a smile. "Uh... I need to move apartments. Don't wanna, but have to."

"Your landlord doing something illegal? Or neighbors? There's ways to break your lease, but there's usually a fee..."

"Oh, I know." Chase sounded bitter. "Boy, do I know."

Jackson leaned in. "I can put you in touch with the lawyer who helped me get my shed rezoned. He does all kinds of property stuff, and he's cheap. Might save you money if your lease break fee is high enough..."

Chase snorted and gulped the rest of his beer down, pushing back his glass. "No lawyers. I'll deal with whatever I have to."

Jackson rubbed his chin. He reached out to touch Chase's arm. "Just... let me know if I can help, all right? We still don't know each other super-well, but I worry about you."

It was true: it was easy to worry about Chase, especially when he had so many odd habits that Jackson just hadn't placed yet. Nothing that was a deal-breaker... just odd.

"Thanks," Chase smiled and leaned in across the table to peck Jackson's lips. "C'mon, let's get home. Your place?"

"My place is good," Jackson agreed. They headed up to the bar, debit cards in hand. Before Chase could pay, he took the bill, playfully shouldering in past him.

"Thanks," Chase laughed from behind him. Chase touched the middle of his back as he waited next to him to leave.

They made polite conversation with the waiter. Jackson felt eyes on their back as they left the bar holding hands. He'd learned over the years there weren't as many people watching as it felt like, but it only took one asshole. Not that

that would stop him. If he wanted to hold Chase's hand, fuck it, he would.

Besides, Chase's hand was warm in his, and Jackson was tingling at the looks Chase was starting to give him. They couldn't get home soon enough.

Twenty~Two

CHASE

JACKSON'S HOUSE HAD SMALL PILES OF CONSTRUCTION material in strange corners. It didn't look quite finished, but it felt... like home. Maybe because it smelled like Jackson and it had far more character than Chase's plain little apartment.

He and Jackson didn't even stop at the kitchen on the way up to Jackson's bedroom. Getting naked together was the best way to make up for their week apart.

As Jackson pulled off his jeans, Chase grabbed him from below to wrestle him onto the bed and on top of him.

Jackson laughed. "I missed you, too, babe," he murmured and leaned down to kiss Chase.

Chase arched into Jackson and rubbed their bodies together, grinding up against him. "Hnnh," he breathed out, his lashes fluttering closed to enjoy these kisses. "Lemme show you how much I missed you."

"You sure?" Jackson murmured, his eyes lighting up with amusement.

Chase let his gaze wander down from Jackson's eyes,

across the curves and planes of his muscular chest. His stomach was tight, his biceps huge, his cock thick and half-hard already. It stood up in a stark reminder of what they both craved. Chase was rapidly getting hard against Jackson's thigh.

"Very."

He wanted to taste Jackson again. He was so fucking delicious, and Jackson responded so well when his thick cock was in Chase's mouth...

Chase grabbed Jackson's ass and slapped it to encourage him to scoot up over his chest.

"Nnh," Jackson grunted and grinned, brushing his hand back through Chase's hair. Then, he shifted himself up to kneel over Chase's chest. He gripped the headboard with one hand and his own cock with the other.

Chase licked his lips pointedly. He ran his tongue back and forth across his lower lip as that pink, soft flesh came to press against his lips. He licked it and closed his lips to suck around the tip.

"Hnnh," Jackson approved.

Chase flicked his hand to get him to let go of his own cock so Chase could grab it.

"Demanding," Jackson whispered but did so, grabbing the pillow above Chase's head instead. "Ooh, that's it, baby..."

Chase bobbed his head down to meet the side of his own fingers, rubbing the base all the while. A cock firming up in his mouth, flushing with blood and stiffening in response to his hot, wet mouth... That was one of Chase's favorite feelings.

The fact that it was Jackson's thick cock was even better.

Chase sucked his cheeks in and pulled his head up to the

tip, then back down onto Jackson's cock. It was awkward going at this angle but he could breathe pretty well considering the size of the dick he was sucking.

"Lemme know when you want me to stop," Jackson murmured. "Or if you have to breathe."

"Mmhmm," Chase awkwardly mumbled around the length, his gaze flickering up Jackson's body. He couldn't even properly see Jackson's face right now.

Jackson's thighs quivered when Chase squeezed his ass again, which gave him an idea.

Chase brought one hand around to slip his own fingers into his mouth alongside Jackson's cock, getting them good and wet. He slid them down Jackson's lower back and between his cheeks to the opening.

"Oof! Bold," Jackson whispered, his thighs stiffening and body clenching for a moment. "Hnh..."

Jackson was hard now, that was for damn sure.

Chase circled the finger around Jackson's opening. He hesitated before pressing inside, his eyes flickering up to Jackson's. When he paused for a few seconds, Jackson leaned back to make eye contact. Jackson grinned and nodded.

As Chase sucked his head up to the top of the cock and bobbed it back down again, he slipped the tip of his finger inside the tightness. He thrust the finger into Jackson a few more times before crooking it to curve around and hit his prostate.

"Ohhhh," Jackson moaned, his expression distant with pleasure. He gripped the headboard hard and rode Chase's mouth. His hips involuntarily thrust back into the fingers, then forward into Chase's mouth.

He was starting to lose control, and Chase loved it.

Chase rubbed his prostate hard as he bobbed his head. Jackson's cock stiffened even further in response. This was going to be a great orgasm for him – assuming Jackson let him suck him off, that was.

"Fuck, you're gonna make me blow too early," Jackson laughed breathlessly and started to scoot backward.

Chase let him go easy that time, but he made a mental note that Jackson might not mind a little more fingering again. "I like the sound of that."

Chase found his knees up by his ears again, Jackson's fingers in *him* now. Jackson skillfully thrust them inside to get him hot and ready for his cock. Jackson seemed to love doing this to him, and Chase wasn't about to complain.

A couple fingers would never be the solid, filling, hot weight he craved in him, but they were a welcome tease. Jackson was *great* at teasing him.

Chase squirmed, his toes curling in the air when Jackson found just the right pressure and angle to make his back arch. He pressed his head back into the pillow and gasped for breath, trying to stutter out Jackson's name. "J-Jah... ah..."

Chase loved being bent in two and pounded into the mattress.

His cock throbbed with need now, the pink length bobbing over his chest as Jackson pulled his knees up over his shoulders. Jackson was about to give him exactly what he needed.

"Christ, Chase, you're gonna kill me if I keep going on about how hot you are..." Jackson's thick tip was rubbing across the opening and around the hole, teasing him even more.

Chase blushed. He felt the flush spread through his

cheeks and over his forehead as he closed his eyes for lack of any good response. "N-No, you can keep telling me all you want." He wanted to arch up and just push it into him, but it was only a tease until Jackson was ready.

Jackson leaned in, taking it carefully for the last few inches so as not to bend Chase too far. When his boyfriend pressed their lips together, Chase kissed him back.

"Show me what I've been missing this week."

Jackson's eyes flashed and he accepted the challenge. He fumbled around Chase's leg to roll the condom onto his length, stroking himself hard. "Ohhh, yeah."

Chase loved watching that hand jerk up and down the huge shaft with the ease of years of practice. Watching his boyfriend get himself off would be hot sometime, too...

Then, Jackson was finally pushing inside, his hips flexing powerfully. He drove deep into Chase and filled every inch of him with the hot, stiff rod.

"Ohhh, Christ," Chase moaned, his body flushing with heat and pleasure and sheer overwhelming joy. His mind spun, and he dug his fingers into his own legs to keep them up near his ears so Jackson could pound into him.

"You good?"

Chase laughed breathlessly. "S-So good..."

Jackson pulled his hips back, leaving Chase aching for more within that fraction of a second. Each time Jackson's cock pushed back into him, his hips shuddered. His prostate throbbed with heat that shot straight up his core. It made his head dizzy, his heart race, and his cock twinge with the need to be gripped and jerked.

"Hnnh!" Chase dug his nails into Jackson's back and bared his teeth for a moment as he growled his pleasure. "Yes!"

"You want it hard and fast?"

"*Pleeease,*" Chase moaned. He cried out when Jackson slammed into him just like he'd asked for. He was lost in pleasure, his head spinning and his mind focused only on what Jackson could give him. Jackson's cock, Jackson's kisses, Jackson's body blanketing him and pushing up into him, owning every inch of him... Hardest of all to take were Jackson's gentle whispers into his ear.

"So beautiful. Jesus, you're flexible. Look at your face. I'm gonna help you come so many times," Jackson moaned. "As many times as you want."

"Yeees," Chase groaned in agreement, stretching and wriggling to try to kiss Jackson harder.

Jackson gladly met his lips, their moans stifled in each other's mouths as their lips caressed and the bed shook under them.

Chase wasn't going to last half as long as he wanted – not the way his body already surged with pent-up desires. He rolled his head back to break the kisses, but even so, Jackson's lips grazed along his neck and throat. It made him clench and quiver, his body seizing up despite no touches to his cock.

It was rare he could come just from being fucked, but Jackson was doing it. He almost teared up with how *intense* everything was: how loud, fast, deep, strong, hard, *huge*...

"Hah – almost – ah... yes...!" He was trembling on the edge against that frustrating despair. He was desperately hoping he could do it, almost too anxious to even let himself go...

"Come, baby," Jackson grunted against his neck, kissing his cheek and lips again as he thrust into him harder. He drove past his prostate. Every time that cock rubbed the hot button of pleasure, Chase's hardened cock twitched and ached.

His own passion started to well up, his balls tightening... Chase opened his mouth to gasp Jackson's name and draw deep, panting breaths of desperation. "Ah... nnh! Hnnh!"

"C'mon. Look at you, beautiful. You feel so good," Jackson breathed out. "You're so tight. You're shaking... the noises you make... Christ, you're incredible, Chase..."

Jackson's hot, fast pace didn't relent for a second and his head was spinning. His fingers tingled, and then...

"Y-Yes...!"

All at once, Chase's body released that well of tension and desire in quick, hard spurts. He coated their stomachs and his own chest. He clenched hard around that huge length that stretched him wide.

His thighs shook around Jackson's shoulders as his body writhed under him. Luckily, Jackson easily pinned him down, or he might well be lifting Jackson off the bed as his body heaved up against him.

"Hands-free," Jackson marveled, sheer awe in his whisper. "Jesus. That's it, Chase..."

"Yes... oh, God, yes," Chase moaned as the wildfire of need swept through him in burning waves and his heart pounded. He couldn't remember *ever* feeling so close to the guy he was fucking.

Not just fucking. Already, this was more.

He whimpered again at the thought and squeezed his eyes shut. The thought made his heart race with inexplicable, deep-seated fear, yet also joy.

Chase still shivered as he came down off the high and gradually softened. He let his legs slip off Jackson's shoulders to sprawl wide open instead.

Jackson slipped out of him, but he was still hard. Chase groped at Jackson's cock to pull the condom off.

"Wha--"

"Come on me," Chase whispered, glancing down to the sticky mess he'd already left on himself. He wanted Jackson to leave his mark, too. "You like doing that? Otherwise I can suck you off..." He could still hardly breathe. He wanted Jackson to fall into the same all-consuming bliss.

He wanted Jackson to hold him close, wrap him in those strong arms all night.

"Fuck, you're incredible," Jackson whispered yet again. After the condom came off, he scooted back across Chase. Jackson closed his hand around himself to stroke hard. "I'm almost there. Just watching you – Christ, I could watch just your orgasm *face* all day..."

Chase grinned breathlessly. He moaned long and low with satisfaction. Bliss sank into him already. "C'mon, baby. Your turn."

"Y-Yeah," Jackson grunted, that hand twisting around the head as he fucked his own fist. The gleaming head pointed right at Chase's chest and stomach...

And then Chase's body was coated in their shared passion as Jackson thrust forward hard.

Deep groans of pleasure escaped his throat. Jackson thought Chase was noisy, but he had no idea how noisy *he* was, too. Chase grinned as he watched, licking his lips. He pushed himself up a little more to stick his tongue out and let a little splatter across his mouth and tongue.

"Oh, Christ," Jackson moaned breathlessly at the sight, unable to look away. He milked every last drop, then continued to stroke slower and softer. Once he began to soften, his breathing evened out. His eyes went from hazy to clearer again as he glanced up to meet Chase's gaze.

"Hello," Chase teased when he saw Jackson tune into the moment again. It seemed to make Jackson laugh, and now was no exception. He wiped his mouth off and swallowed. "You've been saving all that for me?"

Jackson was already red and sweaty with exertion and the bliss of climax. If possible, he blushed a little more. Maybe it was just an extra bashful curve to his mouth. "You've got a fuckin' dirty mouth."

"Says Mr. 'Come for Me Hands-Free,'" Chase laughed.

Jackson grinned broadly. "It worked, though, hm?" He scooted down the bed again and shifted carefully onto his side, then patted Chase's stomach. "You wanna clean that off first?"

Chase shook his head. "I wanna kiss you first. If you don't mind tasting yours—hnnh!"

Jackson's warm mouth was already on his. His lips gently caressed Chase's as his hand ran down Chase's side.

His eyes were closed, so Chase let his own lashes flutter shut and pressed forward into the kiss. Their noses bumped and their soft cocks touched as their knees tangled with each other's. Chase's hand ran down Jackson's muscled chest and stomach and hip.

Chase finally pulled back and murmured, "*Now* you can get me a cloth or something."

"Okay." Jackson laughed quietly to himself. The affectionate look he shot him as he climbed out of bed made Chase tingle all over again.

It was the easiest thing in the world to clean up and climb under the covers with Jackson. Chase was groggy within minutes, his back pressed to the chest of the man who'd wrapped himself around his body and his heart. Jackson was a furnace, which was perfect since he was usually cold at night.

He thought he heard Jackson say good night. Chase barely managed to murmur it himself before he was out like a light.

CHAPTER
Twenty~Three
CHASE

As Chase slowly stretched, cozying up into the sheets, the first expression on his face was a smile. He smelled bacon. Jackson was up and making breakfast.

Oh, man, and today was a day off!

Normally he'd have slept in, but Chase was already wide-awake from excitement. He could maybe invite Jackson over. He'd have to see if Jackson planned to work that day or not. Spending the day catching up with him would be... wonderful.

He crawled out of bed and washed his face, stealing a bit of toothpaste on his finger to freshen up. He'd have to leave a toothbrush over at Jackson's from now on.

Even that thought excited him.

Once Chase was looking cute enough to be presentable, he headed downstairs.

Jackson was singing under his breath as he checked the bacon and whisked a fork in a hot pan to scramble eggs. "Duh dum... cure this overload... won't you help me cure, duh dum duh duh..."

"Good morning."

"Whoa!" Jackson jumped and spun to look at Chase, then laughed. "Ninja."

"I walk like... the night." Chase winked and came around the corner to kiss Jackson. "Need a hand? I'll set the table. I didn't know you were a singer."

Jackson cringed. "I'm *really* not."

"You sounded all right for an amateur," Chase teased. "I'm no better though."

"I'm nearly done."

When Jackson delivered a plate of food, Chase lit up with excitement. Eggs, bacon, toast, maple beans, and best of all, waffles. "You have a waffle iron?"

"Of course I have a waffle iron," Jackson grinned. "It's a household essential."

"I'm surprised you don't just barbecue them."

"I've never tried using one on a barbecue..." Jackson looked thoughtful. "I can do pancakes..."

Chase laughed and dug into his food eagerly. They were both quiet for the first few minutes as they satisfied their hunger. Now and then, Chase glanced up. Jackson's broad frame was silhouetted by the sunlight through the kitchen windows.

He was so lucky.

"I'll walk you home, at least," Jackson told him once their plates were clear and the dishes were in the dishwasher. "I don't have to work today..."

"Really?"

"It's already mid-morning. Half the work day is gone," Jackson laughed.

Chase groaned. "Disgusting. You're an early riser? I don't know about this."

"Always have been. I noticed you sleep in... but that gives me time to cook breakfast."

"Two in one: extra sleep *and* breakfast. Works for me," Chase shrugged. "And... if you're off today, you could come home with me..."

Jackson brightened up. "I was hoping you'd say that."

Chase grinned and headed to the door to tug on his sweater and shoes. "Then you're more than welcome. You can come over any time."

"Any time at all?"

"Yeah," Chase smiled, his heart lightening. No chance he'd have some other guy over anymore. Early days yet, but he liked it this way.

"Okay."

They walked hand-in-hand down the sidewalk, loosely swinging their hands. It was a comfortable silence now. Together, they enjoyed the warmth of the sun beating down on them already. Early August afternoons were pleasant here. It wasn't the terrible, humid Toronto heat Chase was used to.

"This is your building, right?"

The affirmative response died in Chase's throat. He stumbled to a halt when they rounded the corner of his apartment building. He dropped Jackson's hand, his hands curling into fists.

A short, stocky man was leaning on the railing outside the apartment building's front door.

No.

Chase would know him anywhere.

Before Chase could flee, his uncle Jerry's eyes flickered toward them. He jerked his chin as he approached.

Chase was frozen on the spot, his breathing quick and

harsh. He still remembered the words and more that had come from his own flesh and blood. Jerry had taken it upon himself to fix him the only way he knew how: via a good kicking.

For his own good, of course. Because other people would do worse to him if he kept on this path.

Well, years later, nobody had, but Jerry still made him shake on the spot. His brain screamed at him to do something – anything – anything at all, but he couldn't even speak.

Then, Jackson's body shielded him. He'd never been more grateful for Jackson's broad, tall figure. His boyfriend stepped between them.

Chase was almost stuck in his own head, waging war against his body to move or his lips to part so he could shout something at Jerry. His hearing was faint, but he picked up on Jackson anyway.

"Who are you?"

"I ought to ask you the same." The deep rumble of Jerry's voice made Chase's stomach turn. He wanted to shove Jackson away and tell him to fuckin' *run*, but it was all he could do to breathe. "I'm Charlie's uncle."

Jackson glanced back at Chase, and Chase managed to make eye contact. The look was silent but easy to read: *Do you want him here?*

Wetting his lips, Chase shook his head slightly. He could move his arms now. He wrapped them around himself for a moment. He reminded himself that he was *here*, now, months later. Safe.

Sheltered by Jackson, he was safe.

Jackson looked back at Jerry, and even his aura was

intimidating now as his shoulders rose. "Well, he doesn't want you here. Have a nice day."

Christ, Jackson was calm and Chase felt even more like a scared little wimp. They'd been right. He *was* all those things his parents had told him, as Jerry had shouted as the iron tang of blood shriveled his tongue... His feet came loose, too. Though his whole body shook with the invisible pains along his ribs and legs and face, he moved out to look at Jerry.

He had to look his own demon in the eye, terrified or not, and *win* this time.

Jerry scowled. "Who is this man to you? Nobody compared to your own family. Don't let him jerk you around like a bitch on a chain. Charlie, we all miss you, most of all your broth--"

"Don't say my name." Chase tried to steady his shaking arms and he couldn't, so he shoved his hands in his pockets. His breathing still came in short gasps, but it was slowing now.

"Don't you miss Luke and Buddy? It hurt your parents so much to get your response that I had to come alone to find you."

"No." Chase reached out to grab Jackson's hand abruptly. In for a penny, in for a pound. "I miss them because they're too young in Luke's case or too... too good a dog, in Buddy's case... to be as..." How could he even describe it? "As fucking *hellish* as the rest of you. Hell isn't where I'm going; it's where I left. It's back home with you all."

Jerry reeled. "How dare you?"

"How dare *you*?" Jackson snapped his fingers to draw Jerry's eyes to his own, his chest swelling. He jutted out his chin. "I've beat the shit out of guys like you before. I'll do it again unless you leave him the fuck alone. He doesn't want anything to do with any of you."

Chase's cheeks flushed with humiliation. Getting Jackson to fight his battles was low, but it was the first time he could remember feeling safe for... months.

Jerry's next words chilled Chase to the bone, making him forget his shame. "I'll be around again, when this misguided soul isn't."

Chase pulled Jackson's hand and shoved past Jerry to open the lobby door. His hands shook as Jackson stayed between them. "I don't have anything to say to you."

Jerry's voice was soothing again, but Chase knew exactly what ploy this was. "I have plenty left to say to you. Messages from your family."

"Who? I don't have a family." Chase kept his voice flat and dull, though his chest was swelling with the same pain he thought he'd finally forgotten. It was ten times more intense than it had been at Jackson's family's barbecue. No, a hundred times.

Chase let the lobby door close while Jerry watched. As he led them to the elevator, Chase grew aware of how much his hand was shaking in Jackson's.

Bless him, Jackson didn't ask – even when they reached Chase's apartment. Chase fumbled, trying three keys before he got the right one.

Once the door was closed, Jackson finally dropped Chase's hand. He strode to the window and look down across the parking lot. "What car does he drive?"

The shame was back, but worse. He had to explain this now.

Chase swallowed hard, walking up gingerly behind Jackson. "Silver Corolla. It was parked in the visitor bays."

The spot was empty now.

He was gone, but Chase was certain it wasn't for good.

They knew where he lived now. It was only a matter of time before they found out the rest: where he worked, who Jackson was, where *he* lived...

That asshole detective. Chase was the worst scrapper in the world, but he'd lay into Alex if he showed his face again with some vague offer of help.

"Think he's gone properly?" Jackson murmured, his voice quiet.

Chase shook his head.

A warm arm circled around his shoulders. Jackson pulled Chase into his side as they scanned the parking lot together. Jackson stepped between Chase and the window to wrap him up in both arms.

Chase melted against Jackson's chest, pressing his cheek to Jackson's shoulder. He squeezed hard in return, his arms around Jackson's back.

He wasn't gonna cry like a little girl, but he'd forgotten how damn good it felt just to be hugged.

"Okay, I need a drink," Chase laughed quietly. "It's noon. That's not too early."

Jackson chuckled and pressed his lips into his hair. "I think the occasion warrants it. Unless that happens every day...?"

"No. God, no," Chase chuckled. "This was the first time." He breathed in that musky, citrus scent and pressed his nose into Jackson's shoulder for a few more moments before letting go. He rummaged for a bottle of wine and cracked it open. He found cheese and crackers, sliced up a couple apples, and dug in the cupboard for nuts.

Where did they go? Fuck, he'd bought them.

Chase searched one cupboard, then the other, then the first again. A hiss of annoyance escaped him as frustration knotted his chest. "Fuck, I had more--"

Jackson came up behind him to kiss his shoulder and close the cupboard. "What you've got is fine."

"I want nuts."

"It's fine," Jackson soothed, and Chase let his resistance melt again. Jackson was right. They'd only had breakfast an hour or so ago.

"Right, let's go to the couch..."

Jackson opened the wine bottle and started sharing the tray of appetizers with him. Though Chase was waiting, he never asked. Two glasses in, the tension higher than ever, he still hadn't.

Finally, Chase looked at him. "You gonna ask?"

"I was leaving it up to you."

Chase bit his lip hard and poured his third glass. He settled back with it and cradled the glass against his chest. The dry bite of the white wine helped distract him, even if it was unpleasant. "That was my uncle."

"Mmhmm."

"They... were religious. Still are, I should say. It's the usual story."

"When did you get out?"

"A year ago."

Jackson frowned. "I thought you only moved here..." he trailed off.

That was the other part he hadn't wanted to say, but hey. Might as well now. Chase sighed and chugged half his glass. He couldn't help pulling a face. Ugh, it was *bone*-dry.

Jackson chuckled quietly, his hand resting on Chase's

knee. He wasn't judging him or trying to stop him; he was just... *there*. Someone being there for him was new.

Chase finally admitted, "I moved out, and moved in with my ex. He was a biker. I met him at the shop I was free-lancing at. He seemed like he could protect me from them, you know?"

"And the relationship didn't last?"

"He was... controlling," Chase muttered. "I have great taste in men. Out of the frying pan..." When he looked up, Jackson's eyes were like flint. He hadn't seen him this angry before, and it made Chase flinch backward. "S-Sorry. Not you."

Jackson looked startled. "No, I'm not – I'm not angry at you, babe," he murmured, squeezing Chase's knee again. He set aside the empty appetizer tray and scooted closer, resting his arm around his shoulders again.

"Okay. Sorry." Chase welcomed it and leaned into it. The warmth and comfort was exactly what he needed, even if he never would have been able to ask for it.

Jackson shook his head slightly. "For what?"

"That you had to see all that," Chase murmured. "I hate telling people. They get all pitying... and stuff..."

Jackson shook his head again, stronger this time. "I don't pity you." His firm tone made Chase look up, and then their eyes locked. "I promise I don't. I'm just pissed as *hell* at the people who thought this was okay. And if you ever need revenge..."

Chase didn't know how to explain how much that made his fear grow. Weirdly, knowing that Jackson was capable of beating the crap out of his uncle didn't make him feel better. It actually made things worse.

Now he knew Jackson was capable of the same as Jerry.

But Jackson would never, ever lay into him with words or with fists...

Chase shivered again and swallowed hard, closing his eyes so as not to let Jackson see the fear that returned and knotted his breathing.

Don't let on. Don't ever let that on.

At last, he had a good thing going. Nobody wanted to date someone who was afraid of him.

CHAPTER
Twenty-Four
JACKSON

CHASE SMILED AND LAUGHED ALL AFTERNOON. THEY QUICKLY finished the bottle of wine. They watched TV for a while, cooked pasta for supper, and then split another bottle of wine...

Jackson didn't buy it for a second. Those few seconds of fearful glances had told far more than Chase suspected.

Jackson had expected to hear this sometime. He hadn't expected to confront it firsthand, but some of Chase's mannerisms had made him wonder from the beginning.

He'd told the truth when he said to Chase that he didn't pity him. He was also pissed as *hell* at his family – or former family – for making him feel like this. But even those few moments of anger had startled Chase and made him withdraw.

So, Jackson decided to stay calm and play along with Chase's too-rapidly improved mood. He let him have at least a shred of his pride. This was reality for a lot of kids his own age, even more older, and still many younger. It made

Jackson sick and angry, but there was precious little he could do about it.

"You know, since you're over here..." Chase smirked once the second bottle was gone – most of it into his glass. He scooted closer, running his hand up Jackson's thigh.

Normally, Jackson would have laughed and leaned into the touch, but something felt off.

"Feeling horny again? It's not just the wine talking?" he teased, resting his hand on Chase's shoulder instead of his hip or worse.

Chase winked. "Well, I gotta give you something worth fighting for."

Jackson had been cool and collected all day, but that line made Jackson freeze.

Shit. Chase was used to trading sex for protection, wasn't he? "Did your ex take you in before or after you left?"

Chase looked confused at the question. "After. It was just a place to stay and sex first, and then we started dating," he drawled, his speech a little slurred. "Why?"

Jackson bit his lip. This looked a lot like a pattern. He had to be careful around Chase. "You ever worry he'd kick you out if you didn't do things for him?"

Chase pulled his hand back from Jackson's thigh. He looked like he resented the question, but he wouldn't meet Jackson's gaze, either. "Yeah."

"It's not like that with me," Jackson shook his head. He let that hang in the air for a few seconds. The words were worthless, but eventually, he'd prove them. Over time. "You should get to bed. Early night for the drunk, hm?"

Chase nodded, and Jackson helped him up to his feet. He steered Chase into the bedroom and flicked on the bedside light. Then, he sat him firmly down on the bed before pulling off his t-shirt.

"Mm, baby," Chase breathed out through the semi-darkness. He yanked his jeans off, kicking them free.

Jackson leaned in to press a gentle kiss on his shoulder and his cheek. He pulled back the covers for Chase. "Not tonight."

Chase groaned. "But sleeping with you... is gonna be hard otherwise."

"I'm sleeping on the couch," Jackson told him softly. Once Chase was under the covers, he pressed a kiss to his forehead. "Night, Chase."

"Night," Chase murmured. Though he clearly wanted to protest Jackson's decision, he was exhausted. His eyes shut as fast as that.

Jackson watched Chase for a few more moments. When he didn't stir, Jackson rose to his feet, turned off the lamp, and tugged the covers up around Chase's shoulders.

He checked the bedroom window lock, then all the other windows. He had no idea how bad this family was, and he didn't intend to give them any chances at Chase.

Charlie? For the first time, he had a moment to think about that name he'd heard. Clearly, Chase didn't like it. Maybe he'd changed his name when he ran away.

Jackson sighed and checked the door lock twice, then circled the living room. He checked all the window locks and the balcony door. They were on the third floor, but it still seemed prudent.

He crashed on the couch, turning onto his side and pulling one of the couch cushions beneath his head.

Chase needed a safer place to stay. If his family knew where he was, they could track him down and harass him when he wasn't around. That guy, Jerry, had already hinted as much.

The solution was obvious, but there was one problem. The solution: Chase could move in with him. The problem: Chase might feel obligated, even subconsciously, to have sex for protection. Just like his ex. That final piece of the puzzle was in place now, too. Jackson wasn't having any of that.

But Jackson had to do *something* to help his new boyfriend.

He barely remembered drifting off to sleep.

When he stirred, Jackson heard quiet sounds from the kitchen. He cracked open his eyes, rubbing them and stretching. "Oh, man..." His back was gonna kill him later.

"Oh, sorry. I didn't mean to disturb you."

Chase looked bedraggled, but not hung-over. He was putting on toast. "S'okay," Jackson murmured. "No hangover?"

"I don't usually get them," Chase shook his head. "Want toast?"

"Sure."

Jackson gingerly sat up and stretched, trying to chase the kinks from his back. Meanwhile, Chase put on and buttered two slices of toast. He came to sit next to him on the couch.

Jackson took his plate of toast before he leaned in to kiss his forehead. "Feeling all right?"

Chase nodded, working his jaw around with a sheepish look on his face as he stared at his toast. "Yeah, yeah, I'm okay. I'm sorry you had to, you know... deal with all that."

"It's nothing to be sorry about," Jackson shook his head. "I was thinking, though..."

"Yeah?"

Jackson nibbled the crust off his toast. "Well... Your family knows where you live now, right?"

"Yeah," Chase winced.

"And I take it that's not a good thing."

"That's... not really, no."

Jackson licked his lips. "If you'd feel safer elsewhere, I have lots of room. You could move in with me. Just for a few days, or weeks, or however long it takes to find a new place, or to drive your uncle out of town..." he trailed off. He crunched the rest of his toast and set the plate aside. He said around the toast, "S'totally up to you."

Chase looked stunned. "You... you wouldn't mind?"

"Course not!" Jackson squeezed Chase's knee. "I mean, at least I can help you get a restraining order or break your lease, or whatever you have to do. I just... I can't let you face this alone."

Chase was giving him a funny look, and Jackson couldn't quite place it at first. It took him a minute to realize that it was shock and... deep gratitude. Chase's expression was soft and warm. His eyes flickered back and forth between Jackson's.

"Thanks," Chase finally murmured. He set aside his own half-eaten toast and leaned in for a hug.

Jackson was happy to squeeze him, pressing his cheek against Chase's. "It's all right. We'll work things out."

Chase nodded silently, and Jackson heard his breathing hitch before it smoothed out again.

I suppose this can't be solved by me finding him and beating the shit out of him. If only it were that easy.

"Just one thing," Jackson murmured, pulling back. "Something you said last night."

Chase winced. "Embarrassing?"

"No. Just that you... used to worry about your ex, um... kicking you out."

Chase's eyes widened, his lips parting before he tried to hide his surprise. He didn't go around blurting that out to everyone. "Right?"

"I don't want you feeling like I'm taking advantage of you. I'm... not comfortable with us having sex while you're relying on me for shelter."

Chase looked stunned. "Oh."

"Is that... a problem?"

Chase slowly shook his head. "I mean, I'm gonna be horny as fuck, but..."

"Not saying I won't be, too," Jackson laughed. "Just for the first week or something, until we're both settled. I just... I feel uncomfortable with it is all."

Chase nodded. "No, I think I get why. When you put it that way... it *does* sound a bit..." he trailed off.

Jackson didn't want to fill in *manipulative* while Chase was thinking through his past. Instead, he clapped Chase's knee again and squeezed. "'kay? We good?"

"We're good," Chase confirmed. For the first time since they'd seen Jerry, his shoulders were down and his breathing was easy. If not completely carefree, he at least looked grounded again. His lips even curved up in a beautiful smile that crept over his lips.

When he leaned into kiss Jackson, Jackson slipped his arm around Chase's shoulder. He kissed him gently in return.

You're worth fighting for.

It might be a lifelong task to get Chase to see that, but Jackson didn't mind one bit.

174

Twenty~Five

CHASE

"I'll be back in... forty minutes or so," Jackson promised, squeezing Chase's hand. "I'll just grab moving boxes and my truck and we'll get your important stuff moved over to my place today."

Chase squeezed back, then let go. He pulled open the door to his apartment. "Okay. Thanks. See you in a bit."

"Stay here until I get back, okay?"

"Yeah," Chase laughed under his breath. *That* wasn't a problem. He wasn't unlocking the door for anyone after the close call they'd had last night.

Jackson leaned in and down the couple inches that separated them to peck his lips. He headed out to the elevator with another wave.

After waving back, Chase let the door close, locked it, and leaned against it.

This was all happening so fast. Since Jackson had suggested moving in with him, they'd only needed a couple minutes to discuss it. When they'd agreed he should move in with Jackson today, Jackson had sprung into action.

Chase could tell he liked having a plan, and a way to help. He was grateful that Jackson was so determined to help keep him safe. He still felt weirdly squirmy inside about having someone else – another guy, no less – shelter him from his family. He'd hoped he was man enough to stand up to them himself, but... when he'd tried, he'd just shut down.

Chase was fulfilling everything they'd predicted, and he hated it.

He shook his head, rubbing a hand down his face. "Just shut up," he muttered to himself. He strode to the bedroom to choose a pile of clothes he'd bring. In the bathroom, he packed up his essentials. The kitchen was his next stop, to bring perishable foods and alcohol.

It took less time than he'd expected to gather everything worth bringing. After all, he didn't have a lifetime of trinkets to sort through. He'd done this twice now, and every time, he lost more and more excess stuff. He was a minimalist, but by force, not choice.

Chase shivered when he grabbed his bag of sex supplies: condoms, lube, a couple toys. He'd need those if Jackson held out on him.

Not that he blamed him. Part of him – a large part of him, actually – was relieved that Jackson had laid down that ground rule from the start.

That meant more to him than all the empty words in the world.

But what if Chase scared him off by being his usual flirtatious, sexual self? He hardly knew how to relate to men except with sex. As much as a problem as he knew that was, it had worked more or less fine for him in the past. Now he was going to have to get to know his boyfriend by living with him before he slept with him again. It was gonna be downright weird.

Living with his boyfriend. God, it had been a while since he'd done that. After fleeing his ex, Will, he'd lived in crappy Ontario apartments before escaping out here. It had gotten bad enough he'd considered adopting a cat just to keep him company. But he'd never felt responsible enough to have one.

Jackson's knock interrupted his reverie.

Chase lit up with a sudden grin. He'd thought of the possibility that it was Jackson *before* worrying that it was his family. Something had changed.

Sure enough, the peephole showed him it was his boyfriend. Jackson's muscled arms wrapped around an armful of flattened boxes. He had a roll of packing tape in one hand, his car keys dangling from a finger.

Chase hastily unlocked the door and yanked it open. "I'm already packed."

"Great," Jackson grinned. He stepped sideways through the door to toss the boxes on the floor in the living room. "This won't take much time. When do you work?"

"One PM. Class right after that."

Jackson checked his phone. "Oh yeah, we'll be fine. Do you think this is enough boxes? I have more in the truck."

"Oh, yeah." The half-dozen identical, flattened boxes looked like more than enough room.

As small as the five filled boxes had looked in the middle of his living room, they looked even smaller in Jackson's guest room.

Chase grimaced at the stack of boxes in the corner of the

room. It was a beautiful enough room next to Jackson's master bedroom, but... it wasn't where he wanted to be. He squared his jaw, prepared to argue. "I can do the no-sex thing, but... I'd rather stay in your room at night."

Jackson's arms slipped around his waist. "Okay."

"Okay?" Chase blinked. That was easy. He leaned into Jackson's chest and rested his head against his shoulder.

Jackson rubbed his back. "That's fair. We'll just use this room to store your stuff. I'm renovating my master to include this space anyway. We'll have more than enough room."

Chase nodded. He wanted to sink into Jackson's arms and make out on the couch to forget the stress, but work called. "It's almost noon, isn't it?"

"Mmhmm. I'll make you a quick lunch before you go."

Chase's chest felt warm. He was well cared for. "Thank you."

"Get changed or unpacked or whatever you wanna do," Jackson instructed. He kissed the top of Chase's head. "Come downstairs when you're ready."

Chase grabbed his shoulder to keep him close. He leaned in to brush their lips together. The kiss was so light it was almost teasing. Jackson's eyes closed and he leaned into it. After a few more moments, Chase pulled back. "Okay."

"Mm." Jackson smiled. He pulled away again to head downstairs.

Lunch turned out to be homemade creamy chicken pasta. Chase polished off his bowl without thinking twice about it. It was so much better than the boxed stuff. Jackson was as good in the kitchen as he was in bed.

When Chase told him as much, Jackson laughed richly

and stood up to gather their dishes. "Get to work, you," he teased. "Want me to drive you?"

For the first time since last night, Chase felt safe. He shook his head. He could deal with one little walk to work, especially since his family didn't know he was here. "I'll be fine."

"Text me when you get there, okay? And before you leave to walk home."

Jackson's worry for him was adorable, and Chase glowed as he nodded. "I will."

"See you later. Have a good day."

This was what Chase had missed about living with someone. He bit his lip and nodded. "You too." It was the hardest thing to pull himself away from the table and grab his shoes to head out the door. Stalkers or not, they both had work to do. He couldn't pull Jackson away for days on end, and Floyd expected him to be on time.

Though he kept his fist curled around his keys in his pocket for the walk to work, he didn't see any familiar faces. By the time he got to the tattoo shop, Chase was a little more relaxed.

"Hey, Floyd."

"Hey, man." Floyd was just seeing out a customer who'd gotten a fresh tattoo, and Chase tried to steal a peek. Already bandaged, though. "You have a good day. Call me if there's any complications, right?"

"Okay."

Floyd turned his attention to Chase. "How's it going?"

If only you knew. Chase laughed under his breath. "Uh, not bad. You?"

"All right." The door closed behind the customer, and

Floyd looked at him. "Had some guy in here asking about you."

Chase's stomach sank. He curled his hands into fists again. *There's only a couple shops in town. It's easy enough to find me. He probably just went to each one.* "Right..."

"He looked a little shifty though. I told him nobody by that description worked here. He brought a couple photos that looked a lot like your work."

Chase could tell he was expected to spill the beans. He sighed, walking up to the counter despite his instincts telling him to flee or freeze. "Yeah. They probably were. Thanks, man."

"You're welcome. That was the right thing to do – say you weren't here?"

Chase nodded.

"So?" Floyd raised his eyebrows, then jerked his chin in a silent command to tell him what that was about.

"Uh... A few people I don't wanna find are trying to find me," Chase told him. Even as he said it, it sounded melodramatic and he cringed. "Just family stuff."

Floyd paused, his eyes narrowing. "This about the same thing as before? You gone to the cops?"

Chase shook his head. "I'm taking steps of my own." *Like... fencing? That won't protect me. I'd never be able to actually wield a weapon against my own flesh and blood. Moving in with Jackson? More like running away.*

Floyd nodded slowly. "Just don't run off on me, all right? If you need help, I'll figure out something with you."

"Yeah. Thanks," Chase murmured and pushed himself away from the counter to get to work.

Floyd clapped his arm. "Welcome. So, we got a couple new bookings..."

As Floyd filled him in on their upcoming clients, Chase's mind wandered.

Maybe Floyd was right. Maybe all he was doing was running. Sooner or later, he had to face his own problems and tell them to fuck off once and for all.

CHAPTER
Twenty~Six
THOMAS

"WHAT THE HELL? DUDE, COME LOOK AT THIS."

Thomas raised his eyebrow and abandoned the frying pan to take a look out the front window. Cameron was kneeling on his couch, shamelessly spying through the blinds.

"The neighbors are gonna judge us," Thomas muttered.

"Who cares what the neighbors think? Jackson's moving boxes inside."

That *was* odd. As they watched, Jackson came back into view, walking down his driveway toward his truck. They both spotted someone next to him: Chase. The wiry little tattooed guy who they'd all met not long ago at that barbecue.

More than that, the guy that Jackson liked...

Thomas *still* hadn't told Cam. It was a testament to how well he could zip his lips when one of his brothers asked him to.

"What's he moving?" Cam murmured, folding his arms on the windowsill.

Thomas sighed and smacked Cam's shoulder. "Okay, enough spying. You can ask him later."

"He hasn't told us about Chase renting the basement or anything..."

Aha. Perfect excuse. "Yeah? He said he was planning to reno it. Maybe he's storing stuff for Chase, or Chase is... I don't know, helping him renovate."

"Those looked like our old moving boxes."

Cam looked out the window again, trying to get a better glimpse. Thomas kicked Cam in the shin, harder this time.

"Ow! Bastard."

"Don't snoop around," Thomas shook his head. "Nobody likes a snoop."

Cameron rolled his eyes at him. "Ugh. Fine. What do you wanna talk about?"

"How are things going with you and Noah? You two were talking about moving in together..." Thomas seized on the first subject that came to mind as he walked back to the frying pan to finish cooking them lunch.

"Well, yeah. He has to hand in his notice soon if he's moving out in November."

"Right." Thomas was familiar with the cost of breaking leases. He'd done it to move back here from Halifax in May, and that thousand bucks had stung. "And?"

He turned off the frying pan heat and picked up his Coke bottle for a sip. Normally it would be a beer, but he'd quietly switched to pop while his big brother was around in solidarity. At least, he hoped it would help Cam feel a little less depressed about all the things he couldn't yet do.

"He's gonna do it." Cameron was smiling to himself, fidgeting with his own bottle. "Um, he said he's excited, and... we're already planning out where his stuff will go."

Thomas raised his eyebrows. "Oh! Nice..."

"We want him good and settled before surgery and recovery. It's gonna be hard being around him and not being able to... you know."

Thomas groaned. "My sympathies, but say no more."

Cam laughed. "Well, you know, it's been getting worse. I mean, before they told me I wasn't allowed, I was already cutting back, but... we slip sometimes. But, hell. Quickies now and then really don't--"

"No more," Thomas echoed himself, louder this time and laughing.

"Sorry," Cameron grinned, moving to the table as Thomas served them both lunch. "But, you know. Of all the shitty things."

"I bet." Thomas snorted. "Moving in will keep you distracted. He'll want to repaint and everything."

As Cameron laughed, Thomas's mind fixed on that phrase: moving in.

That was it: Chase was definitely moving in. Jackson had only been dating him for, what, a week? Two? Jackson was being purposefully vague, but it couldn't have been much longer than that. They hadn't seemed involved when he'd met Chase at the barbecue.

Crap. His brother didn't usually move too fast. This was... not like him. They were gonna have to talk to him about this.

CHAPTER

Twenty~Seven

JACKSON

"So, you think we should put in rolling doors? Bilateral, so we can open them up to use as much space as possible?"

"That'd look best." Cam was leaning on the barbecue as he looked up and down the length of their yards. "It looks awesome when it's open like this, though."

Thomas cleared his throat. "We can always just... build out our own areas with landscaping to keep them separate."

Jackson glanced at their younger brother. That was a good point. "Why have fences at all? Except for the outside of our three properties. I mean, none of us want our own zones to defend."

Cam laughed. "Excuse you, I plan to keep a Super Soaker by my bed."

Do I make the joke? Nah... he's my brother. Jackson choked back a laugh and just shook his head. "Okay, so... ditch the partial fences and go for a continuous flow between our yards?"

"We have to keep it *kinda* resale-worthy, in case we decide to ditch these places," Cam reminded him.

"Right. Well, it doesn't all have to flow. We can still have separate zones within our property boundaries. Thomas can put in a fish pond and reading nook. I can have a massive grilling deck. Cam can have... I don't know, whatever he wants."

"Noah wants a sunbathing area."

"Really?" Thomas asked.

Cam smirked. "Yeah. I'll screen *that* in."

"Oh, God," Jackson laughed. "Please do. But yeah, we'll each have our own zones so each yard will feel different. We'll keep that landscaping closer to the house and leave the back area free for one continuous flowing lawn from end to end. We can even get a flower bed or something down along the bottom fence to make it feel like it flows."

Thomas quirked a brow. "Flow isn't a real word anymore."

"You know what I mean," Jackson groaned.

"I know," Thomas laughed. "I like the idea."

"Me, too," Cam agreed, clapping his hands. "Almost the same plan with the landscaping, then, but minus the fencing."

"Makes it a lot cheaper," Jackson nodded.

Cam glanced at Thomas and Jackson. "And the yards will be good and open until after the barbecue, right?"

"Oh, shit, right." Cam and Thomas insisted on organizing this neighborhood barbecue. They said he needed to make better friends with people around who might complain about the forge.

Jackson knew they were right: backyard forges *were* risky. Still, people around here seemed nice enough. If not, he could always go threaten them a little until they magically turned nice.

"So, is Chase gonna be around for that...?" Cam asked.

Oh, boy. Jackson sank onto the picnic bench and kicked out his legs. He braced his arms against the table behind him. "Yeah, probably. He's moving in."

Thomas's eyebrows shot up and his little brother stared at him.

Cam asked what Thomas was thinking. "Are you guys dating?"

Would Chase want him to say? Well... they *had* agreed to go out, exclusively. Jackson wasn't going to hide it.

"Yes."

Cam stumbled against the barbecue for a moment. He stepped forward to slap Jackson's shoulder in a mix of scolding annoyance and pride. "Congratulations. Jesus, you couldn't have hid it better, eh?"

"Sorry," Jackson laughed. He glanced at Thomas, too. "I was just... nervous about what might happen. I wasn't sure he wanted to date."

"Aww," Thomas teased. "And he was shy."

"I wasn't," Jackson grumbled, his cheeks hot. What a warm August day it was. He pushed himself up to his feet to start scrawling a new rough plan for their yards.

"He didn't want to tell you and Noah in case you made fun of his *obvious* lovebird act." Thomas spoke loudly so Jackson couldn't ignore him.

Cam punched Jackson's shoulder again. "Dick. You pays your money, you takes your teasing."

"I know, I know," Jackson groaned and rolled his eyes. "Shut up, you two. I gotta get my engineer buddy on the plans for the decks. Come on, show me where you each want your decks."

He managed to distract them by walking and marking out the rough outlines of where their back decks would go. They planned out how they'd join them together so they never had to shovel between their back doors in the winter or step on muddy ground when running between houses in the spring or autumn. And for summer, there would be even more epic back deck barbecues. They'd just have to build it carefully so they could separate the decks later, if they resold the houses.

Cam didn't shut up for long, though. "So have you been dating for a while? I mean, you met at that show, right?"

"No, not at all. We were thinking about it for a couple weeks," Jackson shook his head. "Dating officially for about a week now."

Cam tried to hide his worry, but it was plain. "And he's moving in...?"

"Oh, no, shit. It's not a relationship thing," Jackson hastily explained. "It's... I don't know how much he wants to say, but he needs a place to stay other than his place right now, so I offered him mine."

"Ohhh." Cam drove another stake into the ground and tied string around it. He was marking the walkway to the sundeck Noah wanted. "Is he all right?"

"He will be."

Cam smiled, and Jackson returned the smile with a sincere one of his own. The worst had to be behind Chase now. Jackson could help him make sure of that.

"Pork and... are those sweet potato fries?"

"Good nose," Jackson complimented, beaming as the front door closed. "Welcome home." He was just overseeing the last few minutes of the green beans cooking. He'd timed this meal just right.

Chase looked embarrassed but thrilled. He kicked off his shoes and padded through the living room, his nose in the air as he smelled the spicy, sweet pork chop rub that wafted through the kitchen. "You're cookin' supper for me? You didn't have to. I should be cooking for *you*."

"Yeah, well, you can do breakfast or something," Jackson waved. "Or maybe lunch. I enjoy this."

Chase came around the counter and sidled up beside him to kiss him hello. "You do?"

"Mmhmm." Jackson transferred his spatula to the other hand. He slid his arm around Chase's shoulders and pulled him in for a few slow kisses. Then, he scooted them aside a little. "Watch out, the oil might splatter you."

"I'll live," Chase promised with a quiet laugh. He moved where Jackson guided him nonetheless. He kept his firm hold around Jackson's waist. "Did you have a good day?"

Jackson had only once lived with a guy, and it had lasted four months before he'd decided to pick up and move. That had been years ago. The second shot at their relationship had gone miserably. He hadn't lived with anyone since. Jackson had completely forgotten what it felt like to welcome his boyfriend home after a long day of work.

It was a deep-seated contentment. "Very good," Jackson answered. "We're getting plans drawn up for my master bedroom reno. And the back decks."

"Yeah? Any forging?"

"Just a little. I'm starting to make fireplace tool sets. They're popular Christmas gifts."

Chase looked surprised. "Oh, yeah. I suppose they would be. Like pokers and... I don't know, bellows?"

Jackson grinned. "I can't make bellows, but like that, yeah." He kissed Chase on the lips again and murmured, "Wanna sit down? I'll bring your plate over."

"Thanks." Chase didn't let him go without hooking his fingers through his belt loops. He pulled him close for one more long, slow, soft kiss.

Christ, Jackson wanted that talented mouth all over him. It was going to be goddamn near-impossible to keep his hands off. He *had* to keep his word and show Chase that he wasn't taking advantage of him.

Speaking of which...

"How did work and fencing go?"

Chase grimaced. "Good, overall. I learned a lot at fencing. My muscles hurt. At work, uh, Floyd turned away someone – sounded like my uncle – who was looking for me. He must be going around the local tattoo shops."

"Ah," Jackson frowned. He scooped sweet potato fries onto both of their plates, followed by the buttery green beans. Last but not least, he placed a pork chop on each plate and sprinkled a sprig of fresh parsley and some dried herbs on top of each. With a little extra marinade, the plates were ready. "You think you should talk to the cops or what?"

"No. They'll want me to press charges or else they can't do anything." Chase propped his elbow on the table and chin on his fist. He perked up at the sight of the plates Jackson was carrying over. "Oooh. Wow, those look great!"

"Thanks." Jackson beamed and set the plates down. He popped the cork on the bubbly fruit spritzer he'd picked up at the store that afternoon. It was non-alcoholic, but it would complement the rich, herby pork well.

Chase was glowing again, his worry from moments ago fading. "You really like cooking."

"Yeah, I do." Jackson nudged Chase's glass closer and took his own. He picked it up to clink against his. "To... To us."

"To us," Chase echoed. He clinked their glasses and sipped. "Mm. This is good."

"Isn't it?"

They didn't talk much for the first few minutes, except for Chase admiring the meal. Then, they lapsed into an easy conversation. They talked about forging fireplace tools, tattooing snakes, fencing footwork, and what kind of back-yard features Jackson wanted.

Jackson cleared up the dishes with Chase's help, thankful for the dishwasher.

"I'll help you wash the pots and pans, too," Chase told him.

It was only fair, if he was a house guest, to let him work at the normal chores. Jackson nodded. "I'll wash, you dry?"

"Sounds fair. Put those muscles to good work," Chase teased, and Jackson laughed.

They bantered while they worked, easily falling into a companionable routine. Chase kept brushing against and behind him while putting away dishes. He flicked Jackson's ass with the towel once and Jackson flicked soap at him in return.

"Leave the last pots, you troublemaker," Jackson waved him off with a laugh. "Molesting me while I work..."

"I aim to please," Chase winked and leaned in to peck his lips. "But I'm at your service. If you'd rather I fucked off to the living room..."

Jackson laughed again and pressed a little kiss to Chase's lips. "Go find something on the television."

Chase squeezed his arm and put back the towel, then trotted off around the counter. He headed just around the corner, into the part of the living room with the TV and couch.

Jackson lingered for a few moments to rinse out the sink and cool off. It was damn near irresistible to just take Chase to bed, and Chase was pushing hard. Every little flirtatious gesture and word made that much clear.

I don't think he realizes he's doing it. Jackson licked his lips. *And I don't want to hurt his feelings when I turn him down. It'll still feel like rejection, even if I said ahead of time I'm not gonna do it.* Had he made a mistake in inviting Chase to live with him this early? Especially out of need rather than the usual cohabiting couple's desire to spend their lives together? Had this been about his own ego?

Jackson prayed it wasn't a mistake. They'd known each other for months, but romance had only started to crop up this month – and be acknowledged in the last few weeks. As far as actually calling each other boyfriends, that was even newer. Yet, already, this relationship was one he'd be crushed to lose.

CHAPTER
Twenty-Eight
CHASE

J ACKSON WAS THE SEXIEST MAN ALIVE. J UST WATCHING HIM cook was hot enough. Flirting with him, helping him clean up, getting him flustered by touching and tempting him...

Tonight would be hot.

When Jackson joined him on the couch, Chase let Jackson slide his arm around him. He leaned into his chest, watching the game show on TV without complaint. Within minutes, he reached over to lace his fingers with Jackson's other hand. He squirmed enough to lean up and kiss him.

Jackson kissed him a few times back, and then the commercials ended.

Chase sighed and turned to watch the TV again, letting his palm rest on Jackson's knee instead. He had to be feeling hot, too, but he wasn't initiating anything yet.

After the game show ended, a nature documentary about the oceans came on and Chase glanced at him. "You mind this?"

"No, I like nature channels," Jackson told him.

"Good. You like the ocean?"

"I have positive feelings, yes," Jackson laughed. "It does sustain life."

Chase smirked and sidled closer. "You know what else sustains life?"

Jackson laughed and nudged him. "You're missing the intro."

"Fine," Chase laughed, leaning back into Jackson's arm and rubbing his leg idly. He paid attention to the narrator telling them about the history of the ocean.

It didn't take long before the heat crawling under his skin became hard to bear, though. Chase sidled closer until their thighs pressed together.

"You wanna kiss me again?" Jackson grinned. "You have a particular look about you."

That's an understatement. Chase licked his lips and turned to press his shoulder into the couch. When Jackson's arms rose to slide around him, his thoughts turned triumphant. *I've got him.*

Their lips were warm and soft, sensually sliding against each other. Jackson's tongue tip teased Chase's lower lip. He moaned and shivered, and he felt Jackson shiver in return. That tongue felt so good elsewhere...

Chase sucked Jackson's lower lip between his and nipped lightly, grazing teeth along soft flesh until Jackson gasped. Chase kissed it better. He pressed open-mouthed, light kisses against Jackson's lips until Jackson relented and pressed close again.

"Hnngh."

Chase was pleased to hear the grunt slip from Jackson's throat. Jackson's fingertips dug into his back and his nails grazed their way up his spine.

When Chase's cock was pressing hard against his jeans,

he shifted to try to roll over and straddle Jackson's lap. Jackson pressed his hip to keep him sitting flat. "Nnh?"

Jackson shook his head. "We're not having sex and I don't want you getting blue balls."

The disappointment was visceral. Chase flinched and looked away for a moment, until he felt less like he'd been slapped. Sure, Jackson had *said* that yesterday, but... had he really meant it? A week was going to be *torture*. He didn't even want to think about longer periods.

Or was there something else besides gentlemanly behavior? Chase's fears kicked into overdrive. Nobody had turned him down like this before without having *something* be wrong. He shook his head. "Don't you find me hot?"

"Oh, yes," Jackson breathed out. He laced his fingers with Chase's and dragged Chase's hand across his thigh to his groin.

Christ, *that* was a boner. Chase's cheeks flushed with the desire to go down on it. Jackson raised Chase's hand to his lips to kiss it instead.

"But I don't want you to feel pressured to satisfy me," Jackson murmured. He waited until Chase made eye contact before he went on. "It's not your duty. Sex isn't rent you pay to exist as a person, or a gay man, or a guest in my house."

Far more so than the rejection moments ago, that was a punch in the stomach, but it wasn't from Jackson himself. The words hit Chase much harder than he'd have expected.

It was enough to kill the mood between them. Strangely, Chase didn't feel the crushing disappointment he would have moments before.

He was too busy reeling from the words. How much of his hyper-sexuality was down to exactly that? Did Jackson already have him pegged after knowing him for, Christ, a couple months? Knowing him well for just a couple weeks?

Chase had thought he was hard to read. How much of him was that easy?

"You all right?" Jackson murmured, his voice gentle.

Chase nodded. This time when he scooted closer, Jackson pulled him in and hugged hard.

"I work first thing tomorrow. You wanna come to bed with me?" Chase murmured. He wasn't even going to address what Jackson had said. He had way too much thinking about it to do first.

Jackson wasn't pushing him, either. He nodded, loosening his grip so Chase could stand up first and help pull him to his feet.

Hand-in-hand, they walked up the narrow staircase, Chase one step ahead.

Chase only let go to grab pajamas from his clothing box and bring them back to Jackson's room. They changed for bed together. Even though Chase appreciated the muscular body in front of him, the sexual tension had died down.

Chase was shocked at how much of a relief it was.

He crawled close to Jackson's side of the bed and slipped under the covers, and Jackson followed suit. Jackson didn't even complain at Chase spooning backward into him and lying on his arm. Chase tried to scoot to find a position where he wouldn't cut off his circulation.

"It's okay," Jackson chuckled quietly. "I'll move you if I have to."

"Okay," Chase murmured, shivering again at the lips pressing against the back of his neck. He closed his eyes as Jackson turned out the light.

They lay together for a few minutes, their bodies warm and pressed together back to front.

Just in case, Chase tried to memorize this feeling: Jackson's strong arms circling him. One under him, one draped over his side, Jackson's hand against his chest. Perfect. It was... perfect.

CHAPTER
Twenty~Nine
JACKSON

JACKSON TRIED HIS HARDEST TO KEEP CHASE FROM JUMPING his bones. Any man's willpower would be tested by waking up with a sexy man pressed hard against him. At least, that was what Jackson told himself. He struggled not to grind against Chase's sexy little ass.

It didn't help that Chase was slowly stretching and squirming his way to wakefulness. Jackson's fingertips pressed hard into Chase's arm as he tried to catch his breath and pull away.

"Morning," Chase murmured. Finally, the overwhelming heat of their bodies pressed together faded. He pulled away enough to roll onto his back, then his side. He faced Jackson this time.

"Good morning," Jackson greeted, reaching out to push Chase's hair away from his eyes. "You sleep well?"

"Like a dream," Chase admitted, yawning. "Wh'time is it?"

"Seven."

"*Christ*, that's early," Chase groaned, his voice hoarse from sleep. He cleared his throat.

Jackson laughed. It was actually a little late to him, but it felt like taunting to say that since Chase wasn't a morning guy. "I'll be in the workshop today. You work this morning, right?"

"Mmhmm." Chase covered his mouth, yawned and stretched, looking much more awake now. He scooted close to kiss Jackson.

Jackson pecked his lips in return. "You're a sound sleeper."

"I know." Chase ran his hand lightly down Jackson's side until it rested on his hip, folding his other arm under his head. The morning light streamed down over the bed and along the pillow, highlighting every curve and sleek angle of his slim body. He looked... beautiful. "Hope I didn't put your arm to sleep."

Your boyfriend waking up in bed with sunlight streaming over him? Christ, it's a trope, but it's true. Jackson could hardly look away. "Nah. You're light," he teased.

The mood between them was much lighter than it had been the night before. Chase wasn't coming on during every spare moment. Even now, his affection was... different.

Jackson's carefully considered words had actually sunk in. He was used to his brothers brushing his advice off – especially Cam – no matter how much they valued it. Having this man listen so well had been almost disconcerting.

"Before we get up..." Chase was rubbing Jackson's hip lightly. "I wanna do something."

Or maybe the words hadn't sunk in. Jackson frowned, troubled. He opened his mouth to protest, but Chase shook his head.

"No, no, hear me out. I heard what you said. It... Christ,

I'm gonna have to process it for days. You should warn people before you do that."

Jackson was startled into a laugh. "Sorry."

"It's okay," Chase smiled. "I wanna please you. Not as a favor or... *rent*... or anything. But because I woke up in your arms and I really liked it. And you. And I want you to feel good."

His words were honest and straight to the point. They dissolved the tension Jackson had been holding in his chest. It wasn't Jackson's job to hold sex out over Chase until he thought he was ready for it. It was just his job to make sure he wasn't feeling pressured into it, and it didn't sound like he was.

"Okay," Jackson murmured, but first, he pulled Chase in to kiss him again. "You're incredibly sweet."

Chase blushed, and Jackson grinned at the sight of the redness creeping along his cheeks and up to his ears. "Th-Thanks." Chase awkwardly fumbled with the compliment for a second before brushing it off. He shoved the covers away and scooted further down the bed.

Jackson was already itching and tingling for attention. His body had responded to Chase's presence. Just the *promise* of a blowjob had him half-hard by the time Chase's hands ran over his groin.

"Ohhh. God," Jackson moaned, pressing his head back into the pillow. He arched slightly off the bed when Chase tugged his boxers down so his flushed, throbbing cock head popped free. Slowly, the waistband ran down the rest of the shaft and then around his thighs.

Chase lapped at the head of his cock and licked gently at the frenulum. Jackson's thighs quivered as he pushed his feet into the bed.

This was *intense*.

It had been eons since he'd last had morning sex, and he'd forgotten how fucking good it was. The hours of being pressed against the warm, firm heat of a cute little ass had him on edge already.

Chase swirled his tongue around the head of Jackson's cock. He sucked it between his lips and smoothly bobbed his head down, shifting on his elbows and knees to a better position. One hand closed around the base of Jackson's cock to stroke it all the way down, and back up as he started bobbing his head.

Chase was fucking *incredible*.

Jackson swallowed back his first moan, but the feelings were too intense: he couldn't hold back the second one, or the ones that followed. Chase's mouth was wet and hot and *perfect*.

"D-Do... Hey, Chase..." he breathed out. Chase slowly pulled his head up to the tip. He popped his lips off the head and stroked the shaft. "D'you wanna fuck my mouth, too?"

"Same time?" Chase grinned. "69?"

Jackson nodded. Sure, it could be awkward, but it could also be fuckin' good. Something told him it was worth a shot. Besides, he really wanted to return the attention Chase was paying him.

"Sure," Chase agreed after a moment's thought. "But I haven't, er..."

"You've never done it?"

Chase blushed and shook his head. "I've given a lot of blowjobs, but never..."

"Not even in college with, like, college boyfriends?" Jackson marveled. "Testing out the Kama Sutra, y'know?"

Chase laughed, his strokes slowing before he let go of

Jackson's throbbing cock. He left it aching for more contact. "No. Never."

Jackson patted his ass firmly. "C'mon, turn that cute little ass around and get your PJs off."

It was a mutual fumble to yank off shirts and boxers now as they ground together. Jackson's wet, aching cock kept grinding against bare skin. He wouldn't mind just frotting against Chase sometime, pressing their cocks between their firm bodies...

Once Chase was naked, he slapped that ass lightly and moaned. "God, you're hot. Turn around."

Chase blushed. "Just, like, hands and knees?"

"Mmhmm."

Chase shifted, turning around until that gorgeous butt was all Jackson could see.

He grinned with appreciation. "A little further back... that's it."

When Chase's cock brushed against Jackson's chin, he reached out to run a hand up Chase's side to his ribs, then back down his back. It was always strange touching a lover in reverse, a bit like petting an animal the wrong way. It just *felt* incorrect.

But there was something about the newness that was exciting, particularly for Chase.

Chase's dick stiffened easily as Jackson mouthed his way from tip to base. Jackson gently licked his balls, then pressed a few kisses just behind them before licking his way back again. He kissed along the seam. He loved the way Chase's dick twitched as it hardened.

"Oh, yeah," he heard Chase quietly whisper to himself and grinned without commenting. Moments later, warm wetness closed around the head of his own cock again. Chase swallowed his cock down to the base. It had to go into his mouth at a different angle this time, but it almost fit better this way. The head slid right down the tight ring of Chase's throat as Chase deep-throated him.

"Hnngh!" Jackson groaned, the vibrations quivering through Chase's cock as he sucked the tip of it. He kept his tongue dancing around the frenulum to get Chase warmed up, too.

"Nnh-- hnnh, hah..." Chase panted as best he could as he bobbed his head up and down the shaft awkwardly.

It was sort of the wrong angle, especially now that Chase was hard, but Jackson was determined to make it work. He reached up to grab Chase's thighs and keep him steady, and Chase moaned.

Oh, *fuck*, the vibrations felt incredible! Jackson treated Chase to a groan in return. Their noises quickly started to come with every bob and suck in an incredible feedback loop.

Chase stumbled now and then, losing his balance over Jackson. Jackson gripped his thighs hard to keep him in place and bobbed his head as best he could from underneath.

When Chase pulled his mouth off Jackson's cock, Jackson gasped around Chase's cock. He pulled his head up, licking rapid circles around the tip.

"*Fuck*, Jackson, s'too hard to... focus when you – hnnh! When you do that! Christ. Oh, fuck, yes...!" Chase whimpered, his thighs already tensing up and trembling.

It was gonna be easy to see when he was ready to come, at least.

Jackson redoubled his efforts, sucking harder on the tip. He kept swirling his tongue as he twisted his hand up and down the shaft.

Chase's thickness swelled in his hand and between his lips. Then, Chase was coating his throat with sticky, warm passion that Jackson loved swallowing. Each little lick of his tongue as he swallowed made Chase's hips snap forward again. The hard, warm flesh sliding across his tongue was addictive.

"Ohhh, God," Chase whimpered, rubbing his cheek along Jackson's achingly-hard dick. "Oh my god, I didn't warn you, s-sorry... oh, Christ, that's amazing. Don't stop... please..."

Jackson bobbed his head slower now, still maintaining light suction around Chase's shaft. He sucked every little squirt until Chase was dry. He swirled his tongue until it ached, never relenting on his firm grip around the base of Chase's shaft. "Nnh! Oh, hnnh, J-Jackson, I... nnh... mmm..." a series of low moans escaped Chase with each squirt and thrust.

Chase had never come so fast and easily, and Jackson *loved* it.

Chase shuddered again, his hips pushing forward to slide his softening cock across Jackson's tongue. He let out a long, slow breath. "O-Okay, Christ. That's good. Oh, God, Jackson. Nnh, I'm... That was so good."

Jackson slowly pulled his mouth up and off Chase's shaft. He was grateful that the awkward angle was over, at least. He kissed Chase's thigh and stomach playfully and carefully rolled Chase until he was on his side.

Chase didn't stay there for longer than two seconds before he scrambled around.

Jackson leaned back, sitting up against the headboard now. His cock stood up straight, the flushed head begging for attention. It was a prickly fire of discomfort, yet extreme arousal. He *had* to come. He was on the edge and Chase had teased him to the very precipice before pulling away to enjoy his own orgasm.

"Whoa, you can take a sec-- *Nnngh!*"

Chase knelt between his legs and wrapped his hand around the shaft. He smoothly pushed the head between his lips. The sudden warm wet of Chase's tongue under Jackson's cock head made his whole body pulsate with pleasure.

Jackson grabbed the back of Chase's head and Chase moaned his approval, pulling Jackson's other hand toward his hair, too. With both his hands on the back of Chase's head, it was the hardest thing in the world not to fuck that beautiful mouth.

Chase's lips were already stretched around his thick shaft, his eyes flickering up to meet Jackson's. They were hazy and flushed, especially when he pushed his head down to take Jackson's entire cock into his mouth and throat.

Jackson had *seconds*, if even that.

"Ch-Chase, I – Chase, I'm gonna... holy shit... don't stop..." Jackson echoed Chase's words from just a minute ago, his eyes squeezing shut. Days of tension were clenching his thighs and stomach and arms. His hands tightened in Chase's hair. Chase swiped his tongue and swirled and moaned, even swallowed his cock down...

Then, blissful blackness and climax. Jackson gasped, his arms and legs tensing with super-strength. He had an absolute focus on *Chase*, and every bit of how goddamn fucking incredibly *sexy* he was. His cock tasted incredible, his orgasms were the hottest to witness, and the way he moaned and whimpered uncontrollably when he came...

Chase swallowed hard with each squirt, his hand twisting around the base of Jackson's cock. He swiped his tongue under the head and sucked, bobbing his head just a little.

When Jackson cracked his eyes, Chase was watching him with distant, hooded eyes and flushed cheeks. His bedhead hair was even more messy now with Jackson's hands carding through it.

Chase was stunning, and he didn't even know it. Jackson had the air sucked right out of his lungs as he desperately quivered those last few times.

The tension drained from him and Jackson let out long, deep sighs of pleasure. Chase licked him a few more times before pulling back.

They didn't say anything for a few moments. Chase drew himself up to kneel across Jackson's lap and kiss him.

Jackson didn't give a damn that they could taste each other. He just wanted to crush Chase against him, hug him, and maybe sleep with him all day to recover from those mind-blowing climaxes.

"Nnnh," Chase moaned quietly when Jackson's lips caressed his. Their bodies melted together in mutual pleasure.

Finally, Jackson pulled back for breath. "Christ, Chase. 69ing is supposed to be awkward, not the hottest thing I've ever done."

Chase pulled back and laughed loudly, his cheeks still flushed with pleasure.

Jackson let his hand run down Chase's chest, his fingers tracing his tattoo across his pec and his bare stomach. He touched Chase's smooth, colorful arms as Chase rested against him.

Jackson pressed his face into Chase's neck and murmured, "We gotta shower before you get to work."

"Oh, don't remind me of work," Chase mumbled. "I was just planning round two."

Jackson chuckled deeply and ran his hand down Chase's back to cup that cute little ass. "It'll give you more time to daydream about next time."

"Mm. Perfect." Chase finally peeled himself away from Jackson, reaching out to pull Jackson to his feet as well. They headed for the master bedroom shower.

Jackson's mind turned slowly over everything. There was the barbecue this weekend where he had to play nicely with the neighbors. Chase's ongoing situation where he couldn't just beat the crap out of his shitty uncle sucked, too. There was a lot to think about the fine balance they were walking between unhealthy habits and a possible new future...

Perhaps it was just the hormones flooding his whole body, but warmth burned in his bones long before he stepped into the shower. It was a glow of satisfaction; nothing bothered him so long as Chase was squeezing into his shower stall alongside him. Chase was still joking and flirting and Jackson's cheeks hurt from smiling.

This hadn't been a mistake at all.

Thirty

CHASE

Morning shift week always sucked, but the first few mornings went surprisingly well. Chase still had that edge of tension every time the shop door rattled. He also knew he had the upper ground while he was at his own workplace.

On Wednesday, just before lunchtime, something prickled along the back of his neck. He jerked his head up sharply from his phone and pocketed it on instinct.

It wasn't a customer approaching the door, though. He'd know that silhouette anywhere.

The door rattled as Jerry entered. They locked eyes. Chase shuddered with anticipation as the words dripped from Jerry's lips.

"There you are."

Despite the shiver that ran down his spine, Chase stood tall this time. If his hands shook, his clenched fists hid it. "It's not hide and seek. I just don't want you talking to me."

"But *I'm* not done talking to you, young man."

He was eight again and he'd been caught taking the Lord's name in vain. Jerry was making him read Bible verses until his mouth was parched and he begged Father Williams for forgiveness.

He was thirteen and he'd been caught watching Matthew get changed at summer camp. Jerry was taking him behind the shed to slap him until he begged God for forgiveness.

He was reeling from coming out to his family. Jerry had taken him outside, reassuring his parents that he'd "deal with the situation" while wearing *that* look...

No. He wasn't.

"I don't care if you're not done," Chase snapped. "You don't own me anymore, and you never did."

"Where's the Charlie boy we once knew?" Chase wasn't fooled by the cadence of Jerry's voice for a second. He knew what his uncle was capable of, and it wasn't happening again.

He was alone in the shop. Floyd wasn't due to join him until three, and Jackson was at work. It was just he and Jerry.

"We miss you. Luke misses you especially. He gave me a letter for you."

Jerry started to approach, but Chase held out a hand to make him stop. When Jerry did, Chase stood a little straighter. The gesture had worked.

"Drop it there. I'll pick it up later."

Jerry sneered, and *there* was that ugly mask he'd worn that day while trying to kick the gay out of Chase. Chase sneered right back in recognition.

Jerry's hand crumpled around the page, crushing it into a tight ball in his hand. He didn't look away for a second, letting Chase know that this was punishment. As always, Luke was his trump card – the ace he had up his sleeve to make Chase come crawling back.

This time, Chase wasn't rooted to the spot. In fact, he wanted to come around the counter and *punch* him. How dare he destroy his little brother's letter after trying to claim that he cared about him? It was fucking transparent now.

"It makes me sick that you keep trying to use Luke and Buddy to manipulate me," Chase snapped. He lowered his voice to make sure Jerry had to strain to hear him. "I love him a lot, and I hope things go well for him, if that's even possible. And I'll try to help him out of there, too, when he's eighteen and I can talk to him again."

"You think we're just going to let you go, son?"

"I'm not your son," Chase spat out. "And yeah, you *will* leave me alone. I work with a lot of needles, and at home, I've got more medieval sharp things around."

"What?"

Chase's hands shook, but he pulled himself away from the counter as if to step around it. "I'll defend myself this time, however I have to." Chase smiled bitterly and jutted his chin out. He knew what would fuck with Jerry's head. "Do not think that I came to bring peace on the earth; I did not come to bring peace, but a sword."

For the first time in his memory, Jerry looked unnerved enough to take a step back. Just one, but it was enough to bolster Chase's confidence. His hands still shook, but his heart burned.

"How dare you?" Jerry whispered.

Do not fear those who kill the body but are unable to kill the soul; but rather fear him who is able to destroy both soul and body in hell. Another quote from that same chapter filled Chase's mind. A Biblical verse was the last thing he'd expected to give him a sense of utter calm, but Chase wasn't questioning it.

The fear quelled away to nothing, and that left space for a shudder of rage to course through Chase. He wasn't frozen now; he was white-hot in anger. He *was* the metal freshly drawn from Jackson's forge.

"You're going to hell," Jerry breathed out, his voice a taunt and a threat, not a warning.

Rather than dread and anguish, Chase just felt bitter satisfaction. "Good. All the best people will be there, and hopefully you won't be. Or, if God is good, you will be. I can't *wait* to see you there."

Jerry's eyes narrowed in that hideous anger. Chase stood tall as he walked out from around the counter, his fists near his sides. "Get out. Don't ever, *ever* approach or communicate or talk to me again. The same goes for my parents so long as they blindly swallow what they're told. Tell Luke and Buddy I love them, if you have any shred of conscience left. And get... the *fuck*... out of Fredericton."

Jerry hauled back and Chase tensed. Rather than a fist, a wad of paper – Luke's letter – hit Chase's chest and bounced to the ground. Chase stood firm and didn't flinch.

He could never remember Jerry being the first to back down. Ever. And the way Jerry watched him... He saw him as a man now, not a kid in need of taming.

"You uttered a threat. I'll call the cops on you."

"Fine," Chase told him. "But not the ones here, because you're on your way out of town, right?" he taunted. "I don't care if you get the whole Ontario RCMP out looking for me, 'cause I'm not going back there for love nor money. I don't have anything there for me."

"Your family--"

"I don't have one," Chase told him, his voice harsher. Jerry recoiled again, and Chase jutted his chin out. "Now leave."

There were a few long seconds of silence. Jerry stepped back and gripped the door handle. "You can't take this back.

Even if you repent, you will never be welcome on the MacLeod doorstep again, Charles."

"Good," Chase told him, and he meant it. He might be shaking, his stomach might be sick from anxiety, but *he was free*. "Because I'm not a MacLeod, or a Charles, anymore. And I'm a better man for it, and a thousand times happier. I'm not there yet, but I'm getting better."

And it was true. Chase's chest swelled with pride in himself, for the first time he could remember. He *was* getting better. He was slowly working on it. And even drunk as a skunk, high off the music, fucking strangers in their backseats, he'd been far happier than he ever had been back there.

"Goodbye." Jerry's voice was empty as he turned his back and yanked open the shop door.

Chase kept his fists ready, just in case this was a feint, but there was a finality to Jerry's voice. There was a complete shutdown in emotion and recognition that he'd never heard before. It was like Jerry was talking to a stranger, not his own nephew. "Goodbye."

Jerry strode down the street without a backward glance.

For a long minute, Chase just stood there, his chest rising and falling rapidly.

All it had taken, all this time, was to threaten his uncle with a sword? Finally, he started to laugh at that bizarre fact – at how over-the-top it was, how fucking *weird* his life was. He sank into a waiting area chair, still laughing so hard he doubled over on his knees, tears stinging his eyes.

A sword. A fuckin' sword. He'd threatened to fuckin' *stab* his *uncle* with a medieval weapon he'd promised Jackson not to use! One he didn't even *own* yet – that wasn't even *forged* yet! And tattoo machine needles!

The hysterical laughter he couldn't stop was the kind

came with utter, absolute closure, with emotion he hardly knew how to process. He latched onto the weirdest thing he could think of – that goddamn sword – and laughed until he cried.

It took Chase a few minutes before he could breathe again, still doubled over on his knees.

"He who has lost his life for my sake will find it." He licked his lips as he straightened up, then tried to dismiss the verses from his head.

Finally, his eyes were drawn to the wad of paper on the floor. He forced himself to get up and scoop up the paper, and walked over to the counter to smooth it out.

It wasn't a letter at all, but a crayon drawing, slightly better than stick figures but not advanced yet. One man had too-long arms and legs and colorful scrawls across them. The other figure next to him was shorter and had curly black hair – just like Luke always drew himself. They both smiled.

Chase's eyes were drawn to the backdrop, and their family church standing in the background. The cross on the roof overshadowed the rest of the drawing.

"Oh, Luke," he murmured, rubbing a thumb along the lines. "Church isn't the only road to salvation." His brother was young; he had years to learn that. Chase prayed he'd be able to find some way to help him along in the next eight years, before he was free from their family.

Chase bit his lip hard and folded the page, tucking it into his pocket. He could see customers approaching from across the street, and he had to be normal. Somewhat normal. At least he wasn't distraught like he'd once thought he would be in this moment.

He was just... empty.

If this was a victory, why did it feel so much like losing?

By the time the customers were gone, Chase's heart rate had steadied and he felt almost dizzy. The stress of the last few days was gone. Instead of relief, it left him feeling anxious. It was like he needed something to worry about instead.

He pulled out his phone to send Jackson a text.

Jerry came in & I talked to him. He should leave me alone now.

Jackson's response came before he could even put his phone away.

I'll pick you up after work. 5?

Chase smiled to himself. Jackson was worried for his safety, but he didn't have to be. Chase had this weird feeling that... that was it. Jerry had never sounded so final.

Yep 5. OK.

He went to tuck his phone away again and his finger brushed a sharp corner in his pocket. When he pulled out the business card, his eyebrows raised.

He needed to do laundry. But more than that, this must have been the pair of jeans he was wearing the day Alex had come in to confess what he'd done.

And suddenly, Chase had an idea what he could do for him.

Alex picked up right away. "Hello?"

"This is Chase. About that favor..."

Alex rustled in the background and paid attention. "Yes?"

"My uncle, Jerry MacLeod, came to find me. Make sure he's left town for good, and that nobody else is coming."

"Okay, I can do that." Alex was already typing in the background. "Er, Chase?"

"Yeah?"

"Thank you for letting me help out. I... This is the least I can do."

"I'm not here to appease your conscience," Chase muttered. It was more grumpy than truly bitter. Alex *had* been doing his job; it was just kind of an asshole job. "Just tell me if they're gone for good."

"I'll come see you this weekend – sooner if I find out that they're around."

"Okay. Bye."

Chase tucked his phone and the business card in his pocket next to the drawing and leaned heavily on the counter. It was odd not to have that fear in the back of his mind – the sickening worry that *someone* would come for him someday. Jerry was gone, Will wasn't the stalking type, and the rest of his family sounded like they were gone now, too.

He had nothing to run from. All he could do was move forward.

Maybe he'd go out for supper with Jackson tonight and treat *him* this time. Chase smiled, nibbling his thumbnail absently. Jackson might like that. Either way, he'd make Jackson let him pay. It was really the least he could do.

Thirty-One

JACKSON

"Hey, good-looking."

"Hi," Chase grinned. The tattoo shop door swung shut behind him and he joined Jackson on the sidewalk. He slipped his hand into Jackson's and stretched up to kiss him.

Jackson loved that he was a couple inches shorter. Not short enough to be a hassle, but short enough that he could stretch up on his toes and tease Chase. He could make him work for a kiss now and then.

Not today, though. He wanted everything to come easy to Chase after the kind of day he'd had.

"Feel like going out for a meal?" Chase asked.

"Oh. Sure," Jackson nodded. He hadn't expected Chase to be up for going out, but then, he had no idea how that confrontation had gone earlier. "Where?"

"The fancy new place down the street?"

Jackson nodded. "What's the occasion? Other than... you know." *Do I ask about it yet?*

"Being free," Chase said. He took Jackson's hand and led him down the street. "How was your day?"

"Nowhere near as eventful as yours... as usual," Jackson chuckled. "It never seems to be. Er, there was an argument with a builder, but the paperwork's on my side so we settled it quickly."

"Over what?"

Jackson grimaced. "Money. It always gets ugly around that. I've never had trouble with him before, but I think he's getting forgetful... He wanted to pay me half what he agreed on upfront and the rest later, but I have bills from my suppliers to pay, too."

Chase frowned and squeezed his hand. "Yeah. And you took care of it?"

"Yep." Jackson bumped his hip lightly against Chase's to make him smile. "He remembered when we went over the paperwork we did last year for his first order and apologized a lot."

"Good." Chase laced his fingers with Jackson's. "So I might as well tell you how it went down..."

"If you want," Jackson nodded. "Not if it'll stress you out again, though."

When Chase looked at him, Jackson spotted something a little different in his eyes. His mood was light and cheery again. God, it had been weeks since he'd seen Chase look this carefree – if he *ever* had. "It won't stress me out."

"No? Okay. You look... good."

Chase smiled. "Thanks. So, Jerry came in and told me he wanted to talk to me, and I said he's not allowed to anymore. He gave me a note from my brother and I pretty much told him I'm out of the family for good. Or he told me. Either way, we agreed on that much."

Jackson couldn't imagine being told that and still being

able to smile. Chase's family was so different. *Shitty*, he wanted to think. He winced and nodded.

"I got a little more Biblical than that on him, but it worked. I really think he's gone for good now."

Jackson nodded. "And that's what you wanted?"

Chase was silent for a minute as they walked – long enough that Jackson started to question whether he'd heard. Before he could repeat it, Chase swung their hands lightly and nodded. "I think so."

Jackson paused at the crosswalk when the green walking man turned red and leaned in to kiss Chase's lips in a little peck. "Okay."

Chase leaned into him and smiled, kissing him back before murmuring, "Thanks for asking."

"You wanna dance after dinner? Have a drink?" Jackson suggested. He could help Chase make this a celebration.

Chase lit up with a smile, those beautiful white teeth flashing as his eyes brightened. The light turned green. They pulled away from each other, still holding hands, to start walking. "Yeah. That sounds great."

"Okay, it's on," Jackson smiled, swinging their hands lightly. "Oh, there's the restaurant."

They didn't discuss Chase's family again. Instead, Jackson asked Chase about his clients that day, what tattoos he was drawing or planning, and about his fencing classes. Chase even managed to sneak to the bar and pay before Jackson could even ask for the bill.

After supper, they ambled back down the street to the gay club. Chase stood tall as he led Jackson inside and paid their cover.

Chase and Jackson stood at one of a few small tables around the edge of the dance floor to watch people for a bit.

They had to stand close together to hear each other, but Jackson wasn't complaining. He liked having an arm around Chase's shoulders anyway, and Chase seemed to find it amusing.

"Have you been here a lot?" Chase asked, turning his lips to Jackson's ear.

Jackson shook his head. "Not in months. Maybe a year...?"

Chase's eyebrows shot up. "Ah. Wow."

"I'm not sure I remember how to dance," Jackson laughed.

Chase winked and sidled closer to kiss his jaw. "I'll remind you."

Jackson finished his drink and waited for Chase to finish his. He led him to the dance floor to sidle close under the lights, his arms around Chase's waist.

They spent hours on the dance floor without having another drink, just losing themselves in movement and music. They could grind and dance dirty for some songs and act silly other times without judgment. If they were being judged, neither of them noticed or cared.

Only when Jackson's feet started to hurt did he nudge Chase, leaning down to his ear. "You wanna go home?"

"I've been waiting for you to ask for hours," Chase teased, kissing his neck and slinging an arm around his shoulders. They tried to slip through the small crowd in the even smaller club. At coat check, Chase gave a startled glance to a tall, curly-haired man nearby.

"Oh, hi."

"Hello..." The stranger eyed Jackson for a moment before looking back at Chase. "How are you?"

"Good," Chase answered, leaning on the counter and handing over his ticket to the attendant. "You? Settling in well?"

"Yes, thank you." He sounded Italian.

Chase waved between them. "Antonio, this is my boyfriend Jackson. Jackson, Antonio."

Antonio gave Chase another moment's surprised glance. He smiled at Jackson and reaching out to awkwardly shake hands.

Another man slipped in beside them and rested a hand on Antonio's shoulder. He was short and round and had an adorable smile and a bright pink shirt. He was the kind of gay man Jackson saw coming from across the city, let alone the room. "Got our coats, Tony?"

"They found yours without trouble. Mine is less distinctive."

Jackson grinned at the bright purple jacket that Antonio handed over to the newcomer. He glanced at Chase, who was smiling without a hint of discomfort.

"Here you are. Sorry for the wait." The attendant handed over Antonio's coat first, then Chase's and Jackson's.

Chase slid a bill into the jar and nodded. "See you around, I'm sure," he told Antonio with a wave, then nodded at Antonio's partner.

"Bye," Antonio bade them, and Jackson followed his lover out to the street.

"Who were they?" Jackson asked.

Chase just smiled at him, buttoning up his jacket before taking Jackson's hand again. "Doesn't matter anymore. Let's go home."

Jackson was happy to fulfill Chase's request.

"Oh man, I'm gonna hurt tomorrow," Chase lamented. "I haven't been there in... *weeks* now."

"Weeks?" Jackson laughed, slipping his shirt off and tossing it into the laundry basket. "What, like a week or two? Try months and months. Years."

"It's not my fault you're antisocial," Chase smirked.

Jackson laughed. "I'm not, you know that. I'm just... anti-stranger-social."

"True. That's different," Chase agreed. He tossed his own clothes in the basket. As he turned his back to approach the bed, Jackson stared. Somehow, he hadn't seen Chase's bare back before.

"Oh..."

Chase paused and looked over his shoulder, holding still so Jackson could look. "Yeah?"

A gnarled tree ran up one side of his back, across his shoulder blade, its branches stretching up toward his shoulder and neck. The leaves were thick, starting in pale pastels and brightening up toward the top of the tree. A kite, caught in the uppermost branches amongst the balloons, stretched up toward his opposite shoulder. In script was written, *Kites rise highest against the wind.*

"That's beautiful," Jackson murmured, rubbing his thumb along the tree trunk and up toward the kite. "When did you get that done?"

"When I first left home." Chase twisted to glance over his opposite shoulder instead. "Thank you."

Jackson leaned in to press his lips against Chase's.

Chase moaned quietly and leaned back into Jackson, his body warm against Jackson's. He fit perfectly against him, all slender and firm where Jackson was muscled. The bright colors and black tattoos streaked across his skin were works of art on an already beautiful body.

"It's perfect," Jackson murmured, rubbing Chase's chest now.

"Can we shower together? I'd like that, after... today."

Jackson let out a quiet breath of relief and nodded. "Okay." He trusted Chase to know what he needed, and if that was warmth and closeness...

Jackson wrapped his hands around Chase's backside to pick him up and carry him the few steps toward the master bathroom. Chase laughed with surprise and Jackson winked, easing him to his feet on the bathroom tiles.

"What a romantic," Chase teased, his eyes aglow from the hours of dancing and flirting. Jackson wanted to show his... love.

Oh, it was way too soon for that. Jackson's heart thrummed with nerves, though he knew it was true.

"You're gonna make me wait to make love to me, right?" Chase murmured after a few moments, stepping into Jackson's shower.

"Patience is a virtue."

Chase snorted. "Thanks. I'll be the most virtuous little fag you've ever had."

That was an interesting word choice. Jackson flinched on pure instinct, glancing at Chase. He was grinning. Jackson brushed it aside for now and laughed. "You're a little demanding."

"I know what I want," Chase countered. He turned on the hot water and shivered, stepping out of the way until it warmed up. "But... yeah, maybe not tonight."

"Not tonight," Jackson echoed. He followed Chase into the shower, pressing a kiss to the back of Chase's neck.

Chase shifted and sighed with satisfaction, his body melting against Jackson's. "You could give me the old reach-around..." His tone sounded teasing, though. He was joking.

Jackson's laugh bubbled from his throat. "Oh, you," he murmured, flicking Chase's shoulder as the hot water streamed down their bodies.

"I'm glad you don't find me... too much."

"Never," Jackson promised, rubbing Chase's chest.

They were quiet for a minute before Jackson let go. "Here's the soap."

"I'm... I'm really happy," Chase admitted, taking the soap and scrubbing himself off. "Christ, you were right with what you said the other day. But this felt different. I'm *choosing* this. This isn't... proving anything, you know?"

Jackson smiled, ducking his head under the water to wet his hair. "I'm so proud of you," he murmured. He ran his hand across Chase's shoulder.

Chase was changing before his very eyes. Even that moment of self-awareness seemed to have made him conscious of his own boundaries.

This was a different Chase than the one who had seduced him in his workshop, but it was one Jackson loved no less.

"Thanks," Chase chuckled quietly.

He barely remembered drifting off a few minutes later, wrapping up the clean, soapy-smelling man in his arms and against his front. As he went to sleep, he had one image stuck in his head: Chase looking back with a smile as Jackson's soapy hands ran over the bright leaves at the top of the tattooed tree.

CHAPTER
Thirty~Two
CHASE

Chase glanced at the alarm that flashed across his phone screen. He shut it off and sighed, glad he'd set it earlier that week. It was crunch time: if he wanted to break his lease, it was near the end of August. He'd have better luck if the landlord could quickly pick up a student around September first.

He rubbed a hand over his mouth, glancing out toward the workshop in the backyard. It was great to have Friday off, but Jackson had a project he had to finish by the end of the week. Chase was hanging out in the house while he smithed.

It was nearly noon. Chase was in the middle of making KD and Spam – the only meal he knew how to make that wasn't out of the same package. He figured combining two packaged foods made it a little fancier, at least.

"Kraft Dinner?" was Jackson's greeting as he stepped through the back door, grinning at the distinctive bright blue box on the counter.

"Shh, don't ruin the surprise!" Chase scolded.

"Oh, and ham – nice one." Jackson beamed and came over to kiss him. "For me?"

"No, for me. All for me. I'll eat the whole pot... with a spoon."

Jackson's laugh boomed through the kitchen. He let go and grabbed bowls and forks for them. "Thank you."

"You're welcome." Chase drained the pasta and dumped it back in the pot, adding the butter, milk, and cheese packet. The ham was already cut up and went in next. "It's the only thing I really know how to make..."

"No..." Jackson groaned. "Mac and cheese and ham? Really?"

"Really," Chase blushed. "I always lived off... um, this, and Hamburger Helper, and Sidekicks, and..."

"Jesus, no, no," Jackson held out a hand. "Not under my roof. I can teach you proper cooking."

Chase held his breath, dumping macaroni into each bowl. "Actually... I wanted to talk to you about that." He carried their bowls to the table and settled down opposite Jackson, trying to be casual and not anxious about the conversation. "I gotta turn in my notice soon if I'm moving out, so the landlord can find a good student..."

Jackson nodded. "Are you thinking about it?"

"Um. I don't know," Chase admitted. "It's weird with the way we haven't dated long..."

"Mmhmm?" Jackson was quite neutral as he listened, not showing what he thought yet.

"But now that we're living together, I really, really like this," Chase confessed. He laughed. "How long-term is this?"

"This meaning you living here, or us dating? Or both?"

Chase licked his lips. "Both." He hadn't even eaten a bite of KD yet. He realized he was still holding his fork in the air.

Jackson put down his fork and reached across the table to take Chase's hand. Chase quickly put his fork on the table, too. "Chase: if you would move in with me, I'd be delighted to have you," he said seriously.

Chase didn't have words for the way his heart nearly burst out of his chest. "Really?"

"Yeah," Jackson laughed quietly. "If you're worried about being independent, I can convert the walkout basement suite so it feels more like we're dating – whatever it takes. But it's your decision. We'll keep dating either way. I'm in this for the long-term if it works out and you want to be, too."

Chase let out a breath. "I was hoping you'd say that," he admitted. "I want to stay."

Jackson stood up and pulled him to his feet to kiss him. Chase was only too happy to lean into Jackson to enjoy the moment.

Chase sat back down again. "Eat up."

Jackson chuckled fondly and settled down again for lunch. They didn't say much over their bowls of macaroni, but Chase caught Jackson giving him sneaky, affectionate glances.

Finally, Chase laughed when their bowls were clean. "I'll wash up," he told him, standing up and gathering their dishes. "You get back out to work."

Jackson looked surprised. "Not going to suggest a celebration of our news?"

"There's lots of time for sex later," Chase told Jackson. The moment the words left his lips, even *his* jaw dropped a little. He shook his head. "Go on, get out. Sooner you finish work, sooner you're back inside, and we'll see," he winked. "I'm going out shopping with Noah for barbecue food though."

"Right, that's tomorrow," Jackson groaned, plodding toward the back door. "I'll have to clean off the barbecue."

"You say that like it's a chore. I see you patting it on your way to the workshop."

Jackson turned red and pretended not to hear him as he stepped outside and slid the back door shut after him.

Chase laughed under his breath, leaning against the counter to have a good look around his new home. He still had to deal with the landlord, but he was positive he could work something out. If all else failed, he could sublet.

He'd do whatever it took to stay with Jackson, but this time, not because he had nowhere else to go and he was afraid of being found. This time, he wasn't running *away*. Since confronting his uncle, Chase hadn't even had a crying attack in the shower, or a dark night with too much vodka. He was stunned at how *easy* it had been. He'd done his grieving a long time ago. Now, he was running into Jackson's arms, and Jackson was reaching out to pull him close at every turn.

Jackson was everything he wanted his home to be.

"So, what's the new exhibition about? And twenty hamburgers?"

"Make it two boxes." Noah held the freezer door for Chase as he grabbed boxes of frozen hamburger patties. "The exhibit's all tiny art."

Chase hummed. For a show put on by some pretentious rich guy, that actually sounded interesting. "Cool. Why tiny art, though? Not, like, *world peace* or *beauty*?"

Noah leaned in and lowered his voice. Grocery stores

were a prime spot for overhearing gossip, after all. "I think the guy thinks he can buy a lot of it for the same amount as a few large paintings and impress people..."

"Oh," Chase laughed, setting the boxes in the cart. "Did you try explaining--"

"That size doesn't dictate price?" Noah smirked. "That can apply in so many situations. But yes," he lisped, letting the door swing shut and flourishing as he turned on his heel to follow Chase.

Chase snorted. "Funny." He wheeled the cart along. "What veggies do we need?"

"Fresh veggies are better on the barbecue. We'll go back there." Noah checked his list, then dangled it between two fingers and sauntered along next to Chase.

Even Chase was surprised at how at ease he felt around Noah. He still didn't quite know how to respond sometimes, but Noah made him laugh instead of cringe more often now. "Okay. What do they like making most?"

"Asparagus, green beans, corn... the usual. Thomas is a fiend for corn. He'll eat it all if you let him."

"Good to know," Chase chuckled. "You must like being around them a lot."

Noah nodded. "Oh, yeah. I'm moving in soon." He glanced at Chase. "You are, too, huh?"

"It... it's *way* sooner than you and Cam, but yeah," Chase admitted. "It was supposed to be temporary, but I like living with him. And I like the family atmosphere."

"Yeah." Noah started choosing corncobs, squeezing them and peeking under the layers of leaves. "It gets a little lonely here sometimes. Or it did before I met them. Now I have this huge, weird circle of friends from each of them and from my own hobbies..."

Chase laughed. "Yeah? You don't have family here?"

"No. They haven't been out to see me yet, either," Noah shook his head. "But I'm hoping to see them at Christmas or something. We've never been super-close. We're the type to visit once or twice a year and maybe call on special occasions, but otherwise leave me alone."

"That sounds okay," Chase nodded. "The opposite of these guys, though."

"Very opposite." Noah frowned as he stuffed corn into a bag, then chose another. "Help me pick corn."

Chase abandoned the cart and grabbed a plastic bag to start choosing corncobs as Noah showed him how. "I don't have one, so I'm kind of looking forward to getting involved with the Rileys more," he admitted.

Noah gave him a quick glance and smiled. "Yeah? They're super-nice, even his parents. It's just small-town manners. It's really easy to get to know people. I kinda wish my family were more in touch, though... I drove them away a little, you know?"

Chase nodded. He wasn't sure what to think of Noah confiding in him so easily, but again, he tried hard not to judge him. After all, Noah seemed to be trusting him like a new family member, and being treated that way was a relief. He kept his voice down out of respect for Noah's privacy. "If you want them to talk more, try encouraging them. Maybe they just think you want more distance than you want anymore."

"Mmm." Noah gave him a thoughtful glance. "Wise."

Chase cracked a smile. "Thanks. This enough corn?"

"It should be." Noah squeezed his shoulder. "Come on, let's go get green beans next."

Chase took charge of the cart and followed after Noah,

smiling to himself at Noah's retreating back. Maybe Noah was loudly colorful, the type for whom the closet was never an option, but he seemed sweet.

This was his new life: grocery shopping and barbecues, bringing lunch to Jackson when he was off while Jackson brought him lunch on his work days. And getting to know a whole new family on top of that... It was overwhelming, but every fiber in Chase's body told him he was on the right track.

CHAPTER
Thirty-Three
JACKSON

"Cathy and Don? Great to meet you," Jackson smiled, pumping their hands. "You live next door, huh? Sorry for my brothers' ugly mugs."

Cathy laughed and accepted the hamburger he handed over. "Thank you. It's nice to see some more life in this neighborhood. We haven't been a tightly-knit neighborhood in so long."

"Yeah?" Jackson frowned, stepping back from the grill for a moment once he gave Don a burger, too. "I don't know much about the neighborhood. I lived on the other side of downtown for a while, but not over here."

"Oh, it used to be a little closer. Since the suburbs started growing, a lot of families have moved there. Downtown is full of students now, not so many young families."

Jackson nodded. "But this is the best place to raise a family, right in walking distance of everything."

"Exactly," Don agreed. He was a heavyset, graying man with a small beard. He licked the ketchup off his fingers. "It was wonderful for our family. When our sons moved out, we decided to stay here because we knew the area, if not the people."

"If only we'd had these barbecues at the start of the summer," Cathy shook her head.

"Next summer," Jackson promised firmly. "We're planning on redoing the yards until the snow falls. As soon as the ground thaws in the spring. It might look very different by next time you're over! But you can come over anytime if you need anything," he added. "To any of my brothers'."

"Thank you. You, too – I hate running out of things while baking," Don laughed.

"So you're all brothers?" Cathy added. "You're the one with the forge?"

"Ah, you know about the forge," Jackson grinned. "Hard to miss, I suppose. I am. I'm the oldest. My brother Cam there's a beekeeper, in semi-retirement until he has surgery in December. And that's Thomas, my little brother. He works at a bank."

"Are you all seeing anyone?"

The way Cathy asked, Jackson was certain they already knew the answer. Nosy damn neighbors. He kept a lid on his first response, reminding himself that a hot temper wasn't the best way to make friends. "Yes. My boyfriend there is Chase, the one with the tattoos." He had his sleeves rolled up and he was making another bowl of salad under Noah's directions. "And Noah, next to him, is Cam's boyfriend."

"Thomas isn't, then?"

"Not yet." Jackson laughed. "We've both started dating since moving in here, though, so there must be something in the air. Many young singles here, or mostly couples and families?" At the barbecue, it was an even mix of people.

Some young professionals, a couple pairs of roommates, two families, and some older couples.

At least nobody had been too weirded out by them. Canada was nice sometimes, especially small towns. Jackson thought they got a bad rap sometimes, but sometimes they were the best places. Sometimes people didn't judge you, or they'd known you since you were a kid. His old math teacher turned out to be living quite close and had dropped by earlier.

All four of the others – Cam, Thomas, Noah, and Chase – kept glancing at him as he talked with Don and Cathy. He got the feeling *something* was up. Eventually, he excused himself under the pretext of asking them to run inside for more meat.

"What are those looks for?" he asked, leaning between Noah and Chase.

Noah glanced at Cam, who returned the glance.

"Okay, spill."

"Uh," Cam spoke up, clearing his throat. "A week or two back, *someone* called the cops for a noise disturbance. And complained about the wood smoke."

Jackson's eyebrows shot up and he heated up. "But the regulations--" He tugged at his collar.

"I know," Noah assured him. "That's what we told him – he agreed and left us alone. But we don't really want people asking the city to come investigate. It'd just be a pain in your ass..."

"What, you thought I'd bite their heads off if I knew?" Jackson rolled his eyes. Probably true, but still.

"Uh..." Cam swapped glances with Thomas, both trying not to laugh.

Jackson snorted. "Fair point. I'll play nice. More burgers, please."

"On it," Chase told him. He pecked his cheek and ducked away to head inside.

When Jackson returned to the grill, Don and Cathy were still standing nearby. Jackson forced himself to smile again. *The bastards, calling the cops on me. I clearly had contractors do the work specifically **so** it would be up to code. And I don't run the forge out of hours, and I even dampened my damn anvil...*

"So, do you do railings?" Don asked.

Jackson resisted the urge to groan. *No more fucking railings.* "I've done a lot of them, yeah."

"We need our back porch railings done..."

Jackson glanced back at Cam, who was nodding to him. Well, it was a small price to pay for peace on the street. He looked back at Cathy and Don and nodded. "I'm sure we can work something out at a 'friends and neighbors' rate. I'll have to come see the railings to write down the specs."

"Anytime. How about next weekend? We can have you and your, er, boyfriend – Chase, was it? Have you two over for a barbecue before the weather turns. Our son will be visiting that week. I'm sure he'd like to meet someone his age who's... who shares certain things more in common with him."

Jackson quirked his eyebrow. *If he's gay, just say it.* "You mean...?"

"He, er, came out to us a few years ago," Cathy nodded.

Jackson smiled. "Oh. Cool. How old is he? I don't think I know him." It was more pleasant than he expected to talk to these two, especially since finding out they knew someone else he had "more in common" with. It turned out their son was a little younger than him and had gone to the French school, not the one he had. That explained why he didn't know him.

He was out of burgers, though. Where the hell was Chase?

When Jackson turned to find him, he saw Chase chatting to a handsome man with dark stubble and piercing eyes. They were squared off, but Chase seemed to be getting on fine.

Jackson laughed under his breath. Chase had been skittish even as recently as the art exhibition, sticking to the walls and forcing Jackson to approach him to talk. He was blooming quickly now, socializing with everyone. He got along even better with Noah and his brothers now.

Chase looked up and caught his gaze, and Jackson pointed to the grill. Chase laughed and said something to the man, who cast a quick glance around the party. Chase came over to bring him his burgers, and Thomas approached the newcomer instead. "Sorry. I got distracted."

"You're a social butterfly," Jackson teased, sliding the burgers onto the grill one at a time. He took the plate from Chase's hands and pecked his lips. "You'll be proud of me. I'm doing railings for Cathy and Don."

Chase couldn't clap his hand over his mouth in time to hide his snort. "More railings? I'm sorry." He looked mostly amused, though.

"And I didn't even take any cheap shots about calling the cops for stupid petty things."

"Good." Chase patted his arm. "It's too nice a day to get into that."

"How did you know about them doing that, anyway?"

Chase shrugged. "Uh, I was chatting with Cam and Thomas and Noah earlier."

"You getting on fine?"

"Stop worrying about me," Chase teased, straightening out Jackson's collar. "I'm getting along with your family just fine."

Jackson blushed and swatted Chase away. His collar had been just fine. "I'm not *worrying*. I'm just checking in."

"Mmhmm," Chase winked. "I appreciate you 'checking in' on me." He took the plate again to bring it inside.

Jackson smiled. When he looked back at the stranger Thomas had been talking to, he was gone. Two new people were approaching him, though. "Hello! I'm Jackson Riley."

Life was good. No, life was fucking *great*.

"Ohhh, god," Thomas groaned, expressing all of their feelings. He stooped to gather up the last few napkins and scoop them into the bag.

They'd only just shooed the last few neighbors back to their homes. It was dark – which, in August, meant it was late at night. The beer was gone and the barbecue had used a tank of propane. Don had brought over a portable stereo system to play music throughout the evening. Jackson had even resisted quipping about noise ordinances. Chase had had to elbow him hard when it had nearly slipped out once, though.

All in all, the neighborhood block party had been a stunning success. Everyone was talking about the next event. Something this big, with every house on the block, could only happen every few months. They'd promised to try to arrange some kind of potluck for Christmas, though.

"They only interrogated me *every other minute* about why you two have boyfriends and I don't," Thomas rolled his eyes.

"So, why don't you have a boyfriend, Thomas?" Cam smirked. "Or a nice lady friend?"

"Yeah, Thomas. Why don't you?" Jackson chimed in.

"Lady friend," Thomas groaned, tossing the bag of recyclables aside. "If I hear that phrase one more time..."

Noah and Chase were inside washing dishes. With just the brothers, Jackson felt a little freer to ask. "So, seriously..."

Thomas sighed and leaned on the table. "No, I'm not seeing anyone."

"Well, if we're teasing you too much, just tell us to fuck off," Cam shrugged. "Or if you're asexual, or aromantic, or both. Or quirkyalone. Or--"

"Or a celibate who wants to abandon us all and live in a monastery," Jackson added. "Read books all day long."

"No," Thomas laughed. "I'm not any of those things. I just... don't have someone."

Jackson winked. "Maybe you're next." He closed the barbecue lid. "Love is in the air..."

Thomas was blushing and shaking his head, but he didn't say anything.

"Oh?" Cam pressed, noticing the same thing. "Is there someone you're interested in?"

Thomas waved a hand at them both. "You're nosy bastards."

"You *know* we are," Jackson agreed. "Who is it? Is it that guy I saw you talking to earlier? Or... Or someone at the bank? Someone you met here at the barbecue?"

Thomas sighed, looking vaguely irritated but still smiling. "It's someone I've been turning down for a while now. I don't want to say who it is yet. But I might not be turning down the next date."

Jackson caught his breath and punched Thomas's shoulder lightly. "You go," he grinned. "See? I knew there was something going on."

"But no interfering or spying." Thomas waved his finger at them both, just like he was little again and lecturing both of his big brothers while they played school with him. They'd always thought he'd wind up a teacher, but a steady bank job had attracted him.

"No interference," Cam smiled. "So, Sunday breakfast tomorrow?"

"Okay," Jackson nodded. "Whose place?"

"Mine," Cam offered. "Noah's got this killer pancake recipe he just found. It's actually really good."

Thomas nodded and raised a hand to wave to them both. "See you tomorrow morning."

As he left, Cam and Jackson swapped *told you so* grins. "See you," Cam echoed his little brother and followed Thomas and walked beyond, through to his own yard.

Noah had already headed into Cam's house, leaving Chase in Jackson's. Chase was wiping down the counters and tidying up the kitchen. Jackson smiled, standing there for a few moments. Chase's lips moved as he sang something and moved in time to his own unheard beat.

CHAPTER

Thirty~Four

THOMAS

NO WAY. HE'D JUST TOLD HIS BROTHERS THAT HE WAS probably going to see someone, breaking a roughly ten-year streak of silence around his love life.

This was the beginning of the end of his stupid self-imposed secrecy, and Thomas wasn't sure how to feel.

He couldn't be *too* vocal yet, though. There was one huge problem. If they found out *who* he was probably going to let take him on a date, they were gonna be pissed off. And frankly, Thomas was pretty pissed off himself.

Still, he pulled out his phone the moment it rang, then waited a couple rings so as not to seem eager before picking up. "Hello?"

Thomas would know that number and the sexy rumbling voice anywhere. "Thomas? Hi." The way the name rolled off his tongue made Thomas shudder.

"Still can't believe I gave you my number," Thomas grumbled, playing it cool as he closed the blinds across his back door. "But go on, ask again."

"Can I see you?"

Thomas paused for a few long moments, his eyes sliding closed. He leaned on the kitchen counter, drawing out the silence for a few long moments just to make him sweat.

"Okay. You can come over now."

"I'll be there in ten minutes."

Thomas hung up and pressed his phone to his lips. He shook his head. It was a stupid move, but maybe his brothers were right.

Maybe there *was* something in the air. Jackson was the happiest he'd seen him around Chase. Cam and Noah were practically engaged.

He had to take a step – whether forward or backward, he didn't yet know. Either way, he felt emboldened by coming at least a little bit clean. It was his turn, and there was no better time than now.

Thirty-Five

CHASE

"Hey, sexy."

The patio door slid open and Jackson stepped inside. Chase put down his cloth and beamed at Jackson. "Oh, hello. I just finished the dishes. All tidy outside?"

Jackson smiled fondly. He kicked off his shoes, then walked over to kiss the top of Chase's head, wrapping one strong arm around his shoulders. "Yep. Thank you for helping clean up."

"No problem."

"You're happy," Jackson remarked. "Had a good time today?"

Chase nodded. The barbecue itself had been much more fun than he'd thought, and he still had a little energy. Plus... "I just found out that my uncle and family are definitely gone for good."

Jackson's eyes flickered, and he pulled back to watch Chase's face. He looked a bit worried and uncertain how to address that topic.

Chase snaked his arm around Jackson's waist and leaned

in to kiss him. "Don't be sad. I'm glad. I already made my peace a long time ago."

"Okay," Jackson murmured. "If you ever need to talk about it..."

Chase chuckled. He didn't have anything more to say about it: it was the last needle in his kit sliding perfectly into the box. It wasn't the dramatic, heart-wrenching conclusion to their family drama he'd always envisioned. It was just the quiet satisfaction of completion. "I think I'll be all right."

"Okay." Jackson wrapped his other arm around Chase, too, and pulled him for a quick, tight hug. "Want to go to bed? I'm beat."

"God, yes," Chase laughed. "You've been looking so hot all day, manning the barbecue..."

Jackson grinned, pulling away from Chase and taking his hand to lead him upstairs. "Have I? Do you like a man with tongs in his hand?"

"Oh, yeah. Except dentists," Chase shivered. "Those aren't sexy tongs..."

Jackson snorted with laughter. "I promise not to become a dentist."

"Good."

Chase pulled Jackson into his bedroom and kicked the door shut. He walked backward toward the bed, his hands on Jackson's waist. "You should make love to me again."

Jackson's eyebrows flickered up. He walked forward as he was pulled along, his hands rising to cup Chase's cheeks. He pressed a kiss to Chase's lips and pushed him backward.

The adrenaline rush of falling through the air only halfway subsided when Chase hit the bed. He moaned his appreciation, grabbing Jackson by the belt loops and jerking to haul him down on top of him.

"Jesus, you're strong," Jackson laughed.

Chase winked. "Stronger than I look, which isn't hard."

Jackson grinned and kissed Chase again, nestling between his legs. They met each other's lips in teasing, gentle kisses, sometimes pulling away to make the other man work for it. The way Jackson smiled made Chase's heart flutter every time.

Finally, Chase grabbed Jackson's back and hip and squirmed under him, trying to get leverage to flip him over.

"What are you-- Oh." Jackson let Chase roll him onto his back, flipping their positions. "Hello, there."

Chase laughed. "Hi." He knelt back, one hand on Jackson's shoulder, and looked Jackson up and down. "You're even hotter from this angle." Jackson's gray t-shirt clung to each curve of his pecs and stretched around his biceps. It had slid up just enough that he could see Jackson's treasure trail across his stomach.

"Thanks," Jackson chuckled quietly. He tugged at Chase's shirt before he started unbuttoning it.

Chase gladly shrugged it off and tossed it aside. He grabbed the hem of Jackson's t-shirt to pull it off. "Mm..." He leaned down to press open-mouthed kisses along Jackson's collarbone, shoulder, and chest. His pecs were so fuckin' firm, Chase just wanted to lick them forever.

Jackson shuddered, his fingers curling into Chase's thigh. Encouraged by this sign, Chase mouthed at his nipple. He circled his tongue around the stiff nub as Jackson's chest heaved.

"Nnh... Chase," Jackson whispered, his voice hoarse. Chase kissed over to his other nipple and Jackson groaned, "Oh, yeah."

Chase smirked, then scooted down the bed, wriggling his

way down. He took his time kissing across his stomach and chest. When he reached that beautiful V etched into Jackson's body, he kissed down along his hipbone. He went down along one side of the V to the waistband, then back up the other side.

Jackson was hard by now, straining against his jeans. He kneaded Chase's shoulders to keep himself calm. Chase loved driving him wild with just his lips.

"What have we here?" Chase teased, unbuttoning his jeans and drawing the zipper down. He hauled down the fabric and caught his fingers in the waistband at the same time to pull everything down. He scooted down with the fabric, then awkwardly shoved it down to Jackson's shins so Jackson could kick off the layers of fabric.

"A hell of a boner for you," Jackson answered frankly.

Chase laughed richly, unable to help the grin stretching across his cheeks. "What a compliment."

It *was* a hell of a boner for him, though. Jackson's cock was twitching, bobbing in the air above his stomach. It looked as huge and delicious as always. It felt like *so* long since Chase got to suck it last.

Chase licked his lips and ran his hand down across Jackson's chest and stomach while mouthing at the base of the erection.

Jackson stifled his grunt, and Chase lipped his way up along the shaft to the head. Chase wrapped his hand around the base of Jackson's shaft and pulled it up to stroke. When he pushed his hand down to the base, his mouth slipped around the head and down the shaft. His lips curled between his teeth and sensitive skin, tongue darting along the salty skin.

"Hnngh!" Jackson moaned, his back arching for a

moment before he settled again. "Oh, *yeah*, you're not wasting time."

"Mm-mm," Chase moaned, though his mouth was full. The warm, velvety weight in his mouth twitched in response and Jackson gasped again. Chase sucked his cheeks in a little more, then drew his lips up toward the head. He swirled his tongue around before pushing his head down again.

One bob of his head at a time, he pulled Jackson along into ecstasy. Chase relished every quiet groan and gasp, every hitch in Jackson's breathing, every twitch of pleasure in Jackson's thighs... Most of all, he loved it when Jackson pushed his hips up for a moment before forcing himself back down.

Chase grabbed Jackson's hand and moved it to the back of his head. He met Jackson's eyes as he swirled his tongue several times along the head.

Jackson groaned and tightened his hand in Chase's hair. He gently pushed him down the shaft toward the base.

Christ, Chase was so hard it almost hurt. He moaned, his eyes flickering half-shut as he breathed carefully. He let Jackson pull him back up the shaft and push him down a couple more times.

Jackson gently nudged his cheek to push his head off his cock. "I don't want to be done already," he laughed. "You're so fuckin' hot."

Chase laughed. He scooted across the bed to grab a condom and lubricant. While he was at it, he fought his own jeans to pull them off and throw them aside so he was naked, too.

Jackson ran his hand up Chase's spine to the back of his neck and pulled him back in against him with a long, slow kiss. Jackson's lips sought out the tip of Chase's tongue, then

Chase's lower lip. Jackson sucked sensitive skin until Chase's nerves were just about frayed.

Chase pressed harder against Jackson's lips, demanding a forceful kiss. In response, Jackson kissed hard enough to make Chase moan and pulled him back on top of his body. Jackson's wet cock ground up against Chase's stomach as Chase lay along his body. Jackson thrust his hips once or twice to tease him.

"Hnnh, I want you," Chase gasped against Jackson's lips, blindly grabbing for the lube and wetting his own fingers. He reached behind himself and between his legs, circling his fingers around his own hole.

Jackson's hand pushed in next to his. He swiped the lube from Chase's fingers onto his own. Chase moaned loudly when broad fingertips pressed into him. He relented, grabbing the bed instead to steady himself as Jackson's fingers smoothly slid inside past the tight ring.

"Yes," Chase gasped, thrusting against Jackson's body to grind his own hard cock against Jackson's firm stomach. The two fingers inside him were rubbing against *that* spot, exactly fucking right. Jackson remembered exactly what speed and pressure made him tick...

Of course he did. Fucking considerate boyfriend. Chase could handle that thought now, though. Unlike the first time they'd fucked, he didn't have that overwhelming pressure in his chest to run away when the focus was on his own pleasure.

No: he *wanted* Jackson to make him feel good. He deserved to feel good. And Jackson was *so good* at making that happen...

Chase moaned into Jackson's neck as Jackson wrapped his other arm around his back and ground against him. The warm skin of their chests and stomachs burned from the friction of their naked bodies pressing together.

Even the brushes of Jackson's skin against Chase's nipples made him shiver with pleasure. Those fingers buried deep inside him were the best part. He lost himself for a good minute of hazy pleasure. His cock throbbed and stiffened into an impossibly hard, aching weight with each brush of fingers against his prostate.

He somehow pulled himself out of the moment and moaned. "Okay, you keep your hands to yourself," he murmured, breathing out heavily as Jackson's fingers slid out. "Jesus Christ. Give me a chance to ride you before making me come."

Jackson's chuckle was deep but unapologetic. Chase grabbed the condom and tore it open. He pinched the tip and smoothly slid it down over that huge shaft before guiding the tip to his entrance.

He sat back and down slowly, kneeling upright now and spreading his knees to brace himself. As the hot weight slid in, filling him inch by inch, he rolled his head back. "Hnnh... yes, that's good," he moaned to himself. Jackson's nails bit into his hipbones. The sparks of pain sent tingles of pleasure through his stomach.

Chase's whole body tightened and twitched with pleasure, heating up instantly with the thick weight inside him. Jackson filled every inch of him. Taking him in at his own pace made his body ripple with pleasurable shivers. "Yes...!"

"Oh, yeah, baby," Jackson groaned his agreement. "You always feel so good."

Chase licked his lips, catching his breath. He made himself breathe out deeply as he settled down onto the base of Jackson's cock, his body shivering again. "So do you. You fill me right up. You're fuckin' big."

"I love that you can handle it all," Jackson gasped. "Come on. Ride me, Chase."

Chase grinned and leaned forward, his knees pressing into the mattress hard. He grabbed Jackson's shoulder with one hand and his hip with the other. He pulled his body up and rocked down again, taking a few thrusts to figure out his routine and angle.

When he found his balance, Chase set into a faster pace, pushing himself down and fucking himself on Jackson with all the energy he could muster. "Oh, yeah, Jackson," he gasped. "I'm nowhere near strong enough to do this the whole time, though..."

Jackson chuckled deeply, reaching around to cheekily slap his ass. "Let me know when it's just too much," he winked.

Chase grinned breathlessly. He rolled his head back with another throaty moan at the angle that thick cock head slid across his prostate. It ignited shivers of pleasurable heat that shot through his every limb, tingling from head to toe.

He lost himself in gasps and groans. Every small noise of approval and appreciation spilled from his lips in a chorus of pleasure. Jackson echoed him in sharp groans when he thrust particularly hard or clenched involuntarily around him in pleasure.

The haze of pleasure settled so thickly around him that within minutes, his pace was slowing. His heart pounded, sweat beading his brow as his arms and legs ached from the new and different angle. "Baby--"

Jackson grabbed his shoulder and hip, gently rolling them over. Chase wrapped his legs around Jackson's waist. With

Jackson's weight blanketing him, his body pressed into the cool sheets underneath. Chase moaned his approval. "Yes... Jackson, please..."

"Please what?"

"Hard and fast," Chase begged. His body sparked with every little brush of Jackson's broad chest as Jackson's body surged against his. His boyfriend drove deep into him, making them both arch and moan in simultaneous pleasure.

He twitched and shivered again at Jackson's hand brushing down his chest and stomach to wrap around his throbbing cock. The ache of arousal burned through every fiber of his body. He gasped and shivered again at the sensitivity. That quickly settled into the pulsating rhythm of desire that thrummed through his body with every thrust of Jackson's hips.

Chase was too lost in the moment to be anxious or self-conscious, to worry or daydream... Jackson was all that consumed his every thought.

He loved being with this man. He wanted to explore every fuckin' position with him until he had the stamina to ride him all night long. He wanted to hold him in the nights and tease him in the mornings, shower with him and cook him lunch...

He wanted to be Jackson's, utterly and completely.

Christ, Chase was in love. The way Jackson watched him told him he wasn't the only one. Jackson's eyes were wide and fixed on Chase's expressions. His gaze was tender as he watched Chase's every reaction to milk every last drop of pleasure out of him...

"Oh, fuck, I can't-- I'm abou-- Jackson..." Chase panted, his eyes sliding closed for a moment as he arched against Jackson. Heat surged from deep within his belly and spilled out. His muscles seized and legs clenched hard around Jackson's firm body.

And he was coming, spilling into the blissful oblivion. He had just enough presence to feel Jackson's thrusts shudder and become hard and irregular. Jackson groaned hard.

Chase peeked at Jackson's pleasure-wracked face as Jackson drove into him. He clenched around Jackson, squeezing every last drop out of him as Jackson jerked his cock firmly and brought him through these seconds of bliss.

"Chase," Jackson gasped, looking almost like he wanted to say something. He bit his tongue and groaned instead, the sound a deep, guttural moan of pleasure.

"Yeah, babe," Chase moaned, twitching as the last few drops of pleasure trickled from his cock and Jackson let go of him. "Me, too."

Jackson smothered him with kisses until Chase laughed, leaning up into every kiss. Jackson softened and slid out of him but they kept kissing. Sometimes their lips didn't meet each other's, but landed on cheeks or noses or chins. It made no difference.

Chase's whole body burned with pleasure, tingles of ecstasy still running through his fingertips and toes. He shivered and rolled onto his side when Jackson pulled him in, finally burying his face in Jackson's shoulder.

"You're incredible," Jackson whispered. They both breathed hard, and Chase desperately tried to catch his breath.

"You, too," Chase murmured. "I've never... had anyone like you."

"Yeah," Jackson whispered. His voice was a little off. "I know the feeling."

Chase pulled back to look Jackson in the eye. "Hm?"

Jackson swallowed, then cupped Chase's face. "You're... I know this is early, but I love you. You don't have to--"

"I love you," Chase told him, loud and firm. He was certain of that. "It might be stupid, but I do."

Jackson's eyebrows rose, the surprise easy to read on his face. "Yeah? I felt a bit stupid too..."

"Fuck everyone who says you have to follow some schedule." Chase ran a finger along Jackson's side, then traced his ribs one at a time around his side to his spine. "I've dated guys for months and never felt half of what I have with you."

Jackson nodded slowly. "I didn't want to pressure you, but I felt it... so soon."

"Me, too," Chase smiled, and Jackson's eyes brightened in response. "We've known each other for ages anyway."

"Months isn't ages," Jackson snorted.

"It is," Chase clicked his tongue, and shut up Jackson's response with a kiss. "Anyway, you said it yourself. You can know you wanna spend your life with someone within weeks. As long as you have the same approach to a relationship."

Jackson was smiling, a teasing amusement glinting in his eyes. "Where's the cynic who told me the other guy could be lying about himself?"

"Well, if you *are* lying about being a good guy, you're a fuckin' *nice* bad guy," Chase snorted. "Which makes you a good guy anyway."

Jackson laughed, the sound carrying in the bedroom. He rolled onto his back and rubbed his face. "I... Okay."

Chase grinned. "Let me have that one."

"Okay, okay." Jackson laughed. He wrapped his arm around Chase and pulled him in close. "You're so stubborn you could head-butt a mountain out of the way."

"There's a testimonial. I like that one," Chase hummed, resting his head on Jackson's shoulder. It was true: the only reason he'd gotten this far was from sheer defiance.

It was kind of nice to let go of that now and then, though, and Jackson was incredible at easing his defenses down for his own good.

Chase hummed, closing his eyes for a moment as they cooled off and recovered together.

So stubborn, Chase thought again, his lips quirking into a little smile. *I like that a lot.*

"There's one more thing," Jackson murmured. "But we have to get up for it."

Chase moaned at the prospect of pulling away from Jackson. "Not yet."

"Not yet," Jackson agreed, and lapsed into silence once more as they held each other. They were sticky and exhausted, but they couldn't keep their hands off each other.

Jackson's hand still rubbed along his chest or side or back. Chase rubbed his thumb in slow circles along Jackson's ribs.

This, right here, was heaven.

CHAPTER
Thirty-Six
JACKSON

"So, I might not have been *completely* honest…"

Chase visibly stiffened as he leaned against the kitchen counter and put his glass of water aside. They were both just in jeans, having skipped t-shirts. "About what?"

Jackson chuckled and winked. "Wanna wait here and see?"

"All right…" Chase eyed him and leaned on the counter.

Jackson grabbed his keys and trotted through the yard barefoot, sticking to the grass. He let himself into the workshop and grabbed the heavy bundle on the table, his heart racing. He paused to pat the wrappings back into place.

What would Chase think? Jackson prayed he liked it.

Jackson locked up after himself. Thomas's house lights were on, which was unusual for such a late hour. Jackson grinned again as he remembered what he and Cam had learned that afternoon. He strode on, though, and carried the armful back into the house.

By the time he was in through the patio doors, Chase's face lit up with anticipation.

"I wasn't finishing up a builder's job yesterday," Jackson told Chase, grinning. "It was... something else."

"No way. Already?" Chase murmured, his eyes fixed on the bundle.

"Yep. I'm pretty good," Jackson winked. Honestly, it had taken days of work, usually at the beginning and end of his work days. An automatic hammer had sped up finishing the blade, but the whole process still took a lot longer than he'd ever tell Chase. His Friday work had been the finishing touches, and even that had taken a full day's work from dawn to dusk.

Chase reached out to take the bundle. He looked startled by the weight, and he reverently laid it on the counter. "Is it sheathed?"

"No. You'll have to find one," Jackson chuckled. "I also haven't sharpened it since I wasn't sure if you were displaying it or what. I can do that if you tell me."

Chase stretched up to kiss him, then turned to pull back the corners of the fabric.

Jackson caught his breath as the silvery steel was revealed under the kitchen lights. It glinted and shimmered from all the polishing he'd done – endless grinding and polishing. The blade itself was true and straight. The guard was a beautiful woven strand of steel circling the hilt and blade. He'd incorporated all the design elements Chase had wanted and then some.

It fit Chase's hand perfectly when Chase wrapped his hand around the hilt to heft it.

"Oh, it's *heavy!*" Chase exclaimed.

Jackson grinned. "Yeah, it would be," he teased. "Not like your fencing foils."

Chase shook his head. "Not at all." He gazed down the

length of the blade then looked up at Jackson. "It's... It's phenomenal. I can't believe it. It's really mine?"

Jackson laughed, wrapping his arm around Chase's shoulder. "It's yours."

Chase gingerly reached out to run his finger down the unsharpened blade. "I'd like to hang it up. I don't think I'm going to be using it, but if we can find an important spot..."

"Like where?" Jackson smiled.

"The living room? Right where people can see it?"

Jackson chuckled, combing his hand through Chase's hair. "You want to show it off?"

"Duh," Chase snorted. "It's... incredible." He couldn't take his eyes off it as he flipped it and turned it this way and that. He kept touching the hilt and the guard and the blade. Finally, he hefted it in both hands to check the balance. "It's nothing like a foil at all, but it's... just what I wanted."

"Good," Jackson murmured and kissed the top of his head.

Chase set it down on its wrappings, then threw his arms around Jackson's neck and kissed him hard.

"Ooh." Jackson had no complaints about his reward. He grinned and nipped Chase's lip, then kissed back as Chase's body melted against his.

Chase finally pulled back and murmured, "Thank you so much. I... I finished your design, by the way. We can go over it if you wanna see... or get it done..."

"Right now?" Jackson perked up. He hadn't expected this offer.

"Hell, yeah. You got my sword done in *blinding* speed," Chase laughed. "I've got the keys for the shop. Floyd won't care."

Jackson grinned. He wanted to get the tattoo as soon as possible, so why the hell not?

"Okay. Lead on."

Jackson shivered as he lay back in the chair, his arm relaxed as Chase's Sharpie traced over his bare skin.

"There," Chase murmured at last, leaning in to kiss his forehead before grabbing a mirror. Jackson twisted in his seat to see.

Oh, wow. That *did* look good.

A lion wrapped around his upper arm, its tail enveloped around his bicep as its mane spread across his shoulder. A sword lay between its paws. A hand caressed its mane – thankfully, this one wasn't a bloodied stump like the original family crest. Woven into the lines was the name *Riley*.

"That's incredible," Jackson murmured. "I... I want that."

"We won't be able to finish it in one session," Chase warned with a laugh. "You might be tough enough, but my hands have to stay steady. It'll take hours to finish it."

"Oh, shit," Jackson laughed. "Okay."

"We're just doing the lines this time, otherwise we'll be up until dawn," Chase grinned. "Okay?"

"Okay," Jackson agreed without hesitation. He shivered at the cold alcohol pad swiping across his shoulder, cleaning the skin. As much as he wanted to watch his lover at work, he leaned back and closed his eyes to let Chase work without interruption.

When the buzzing machine touched him, he was surprised at how little pain he felt. It was more like an unpleasant electric shock than the tearing pain he'd expected. Chase's fingers against his skin were delicate, yet firm.

It was almost erotic in a strange way, and Jackson caught his breath at the thought. *Settle down... it's a long session yet.*

His thoughts wandered as Chase's needle worked – so much so that when Chase shut it off, Jackson looked over. It must have been an hour or more into it, and Chase had been silent and focused the whole time. "Hm?"

"We're done with the lines."

"Already?" He twisted to take a look at his shoulder and grinned. The reddened skin patches around the Sharpie lines must have been where the needle was tracing. "Wow."

"No regrets yet?" Chase teased, turning to sterilize the machine in quick, certain movements. It was kind of hot watching him be so proficient.

"None at all." Jackson's gaze wandered to the shades between the lines. "When are you free to do the rest of it?"

Chase laughed. "We have to either do it tomorrow, before your skin starts properly healing, or wait about two weeks."

"Fuck, no. Tomorrow it is," Jackson told him. "If you're available."

"I have one other tattoo booked tomorrow. I'm sure I can put aside time for a private client afterward," Chase teased. "Let me just get some gauze on it to protect it overnight. It's gonna look great..."

Jackson gazed at Chase while Chase wrapped the bandage around his upper arm, taping it in place. "Guess I can't shower, huh?"

Chase grinned. "Nah. Baths would be better. I hope you weren't planning on getting filthy before tomorrow."

"I suppose I can wait on everything I want to do to you," Jackson teased. He eased himself up to his feet while Chase pulled him up by the hand. He slipped his t-shirt on, wincing at the prickling skin when the fabric pressed against the bandage.

"Ooh." Chase was working quickly to sanitize the tattoo chair and workspace. He kept sneaking little glances at Jackson. "We can take a bath in your soaker tub tomorrow night..."

"Done," Jackson agreed. When Chase was ready, he led him out to the front then waited outside while Chase armed the security alarm.

He could hear frogs peeping down by the river in the warm night. Aside from occasional taxis passing and the sound of revelers a few streets away in the bar district, there was peace and quiet. It was a clear night, too, and the stars were out. Jackson craned his neck back to look up at the sky and enjoy the view.

He was only interrupted when Chase stepped outside and locked the door. His boyfriend tested it and pocketed the keys. "Home?" he suggested, taking Jackson's hand.

Jackson smiled and squeezed Chase's hand firmly, setting off in the direction of their house. "Home," he agreed.

He already knew exactly what was ahead: his warm, comfortable bed, and Chase wrapped up in his arms. Maybe he'd have to adjust his position a little to accommodate the sore skin of his shoulder, but that would pass within a few weeks' time.

Jackson's eyes wandered up to the stars overhead. The dimmer they were, the closer they were to the nearly full moon. He smiled and pointed up at it to draw Chase's gaze, then squeezed his hand. "Let's leave the blinds open tonight."

"Okay. I love the moonlight," Chase agreed with a smile.

Jackson winked. "And I love you in the moonlight."

Chase stopped him before he could step out into the crosswalk. The light had just turned red, but Jackson had been too busy watching Chase to notice. Chase laughed quietly, then stretched up and tilted his chin to get Jackson to kiss him. "I love you, too, you ridiculous, sweet man."

Jackson kissed Chase until the light turned green. Despite Chase's laughter, he still held onto him. He pressed his lips against Chase's and bumped their noses together until the light turned red again. Chase melted in his arms and kissed him back, Chase's hands cupping his face.

Chase was gonna be okay, and he would be, too. Jackson was certain of it: together, they were starting something beautiful.

"I WOULDN'T BE CAUGHT DEAD KISSING YOU."

Thomas Riley is the only one of his brothers who's still single. That's not to say nobody's interested… his hunky ex is back in town. Just three little problems: they broke up on bad terms, Thomas isn't out to his brothers, and Alex spied on both of his brothers. There's no way reigniting an old flame can work… right?

When private detective Alex comes back to his hometown, he can't avoid the one that got away. The only way Thomas is falling for Alex again is head over heels—on the ski trails. But Alex wants nothing more than a chance to explain himself—and prove that he's not just going to screw Thomas again.

To get a second chance at forever, Alex has to earn back the trust of all the Rileys and their friends. And Thomas has to overcome his fears and come clean. Can he tell everyone who Alex really used to be to him? And admit to himself what he really wants?

Swish is the third book in The Riley Brothers, a low-angst series filled with brotherly banter and small-town smiles. This steamy, standalone gay romance novel can be enjoyed on its own, and promises a happily-ever-after ending.

About the Author

E. Davies writes feel-good, low-angst romance that never fades to black when the going gets good! Born in Canada, after 16 moves and counting, Ed has finally put down roots in north London.

He emerges from his writing nest to coo over fuzzy animals, flee from cute guys, dance through the streets with his chosen family, put together fierce looks, and—most of all—befriend local flowers.

You can find all available titles at: www.edaviesbooks.com

FOLLOW E. DAVIES ONLINE:

amazon.com/author/edavies
bookbub.com/authors/e-davies
facebook.com/edaviesauthor
goodreads.com/edavies
instagram.com/edaviesauthor
x.com/edaviesauthor

Also by E. Davies

Sunrise Island Brothers:

Collide

Stranded

Hart's Bay:

Hard Hart

Changed Hart

Wild Hart

Stolen Hart

Significant Brothers:

Splinter

Grasp

Slick

Trace

Clutch

Tremble

Riley Brothers:

Buzz

Clang

Swish

Crunch

Slam

Grind

Brooklyn Boys:

Electric Sunshine

Live Wire

Boiling Point

F-Word:

Flaunt

Freak

Faux

Forever

Freedom

After:

Afterburn

Afterglow

Aftermath

Shared Universes:

Shelter

Adore

Miracle

Redemption

Limelight

Barely Regal

www.ingramcontent.com/pod-product-compliance
Lightning Source LLC
Chambersburg PA
CBHW050339190726
48284CB00007BB/2070